Impressing His Mate

RAYNA TYLER

ISBN: 978-1-953213-28-0

ALSO BY RAYNA TYLER

CHAPTER ONE

Bones cracked and fur sprouted as Jake took the form of his bear, then padded around trees and pushed through the forest's underbrush, trying to keep up with the beautiful yet elusive fox. He wasn't trailing after her because his animal needed a snack—not that he was in the habit of eating wildlife—but because he wanted to be close to the female, to nuzzle her reddish-brown fur, and inhale her intoxicating scent.

His chase, which seemed to go on forever, ended when sunlight spilled through the treetops and a clearing appeared, exposing a grassy shore next to a large lake. Instead of continuing her quest to elude him by skirting the shimmering pool of blue, she slowed her pace, then stopped near the water's edge. Mesmerizing emerald eyes glanced in Jake's direction, convincing him that his pursuit was over and she was waiting for him to join her.

When the fox shifted into a beautiful naked woman with crimson locks cascading over her shoulders, his bear responded with an approving grunt. Jake's enthusiasm mounted, his body heated, eager to comply with whatever she desired.

He quickened his pace, and as he was about to reach

her, an incessant beeping ripped through the air. Her image faded, and Jake was jerked awake. With a growl that was more bear than human, he reached for the digital clock sitting on the nightstand next to his bed, intent on permanently ending the infernal noise it was making.

It took a lot of willpower and dealing with his surly bear to hit the snooze button instead of smashing the alarm into tiny pieces. He wasn't a mean-natured person, nor did he go out of his way to destroy things. He might enjoy an occasional bar fight, but he didn't think that made him a bad person.

He was a heavy sleeper and not much of a morning person. Getting up shortly after sunrise was something he rarely ever did, and so was using an alarm. His bear was even worse. Loud, unexpected noises always startled him, and his animal was snarling even more than Jake.

If he was still back home in Roadsbeary, Alaska, he wouldn't have cared about dismantling the annoying device because he usually kept a backup or two stashed in his clothes closet. Now that he was living at the Crescent Canyon Ranch, which happened to be in the middle of nowhere with the nearest town almost an hour's drive away, getting a replacement took more effort.

Thinking about home always reminded him of the reason he'd come to Wyoming in the first place—to find a mate. The area Jake grew up in wasn't exactly a booming place, nor was it overly populated with females. Even traveling to neighboring towns, though a lot of fun, hadn't done anything to improve the situation.

When he'd seen an online advertisement for the ranch and learned the place catered to shifters, Jake had been certain that he and Braden would finally be able to find their mates. Braden might be his cousin, but they were closer than most brothers. Jake knew that coercing him to make the trip would be difficult. So rather than waste his time trying to persuade Braden to go, he'd used his cousin's credit card to make reservations at the ranch and purchased non-refundable airline tickets.

The punch Jake took to his jaw during the scuffle they'd had after breaking the news to Braden had been well worth it. Jake wasn't taking any chances, so he'd also shared the information with their unmated male friends, who'd been thrilled about his endeavor.

Then, as a final measure to ensure his success, he'd told their mothers. For several years, their female relatives had been pressuring both of them to settle down and give them grandbabies, so there was no way they were going to let Braden back out of the trip. The possibility of preventing a lonely future for Braden and himself far outweighed the guilt Jake felt over his duplicitous actions.

Braden had been upset and moody while they traveled, but that changed shortly after their bus arrived in Waynesrock and his cousin met Casey, one of the three sisters who owned the ranch, who turned out to be his mate.

Braden hadn't been the only one to benefit from Jake's plan. He was ninety-nine percent sure that Fred, the ranch's cook, was the female meant to be his perfect match. He'd been enchanted by the fox shifter from the day he'd arrived but couldn't figure out why the darned female refused to acknowledge their connection. She and her animal had to be experiencing the same magnetic draw that he did. Fred didn't ignore him completely, but she made sure they were never alone, and the only conversations they had usually involved others in the room.

When Braden first met Casey, he hadn't been absolutely sure of their connection either. Not until they'd accidentally touched and something sparked between them. So, today, Jake was determined to find out for sure, then ask Fred why she'd been avoiding him. Wondering if he'd inadvertently done something to push her away was making him crazy and irritating his bear. The animal was already convinced that Fred belonged with them and spent most of his time grumbling that Jake needed to do something about it. And soon.

The thought of seeing Fred was the only motivation Jake needed to toss aside the covers and roll out of bed before the alarm could go off again.

Up until now, getting her alone had been more difficult than he'd anticipated, which was why, after showering and getting dressed, he was sneaking around the property intent on catching her before she started her workday.

Fred rarely deviated from her schedule. If she wasn't preparing food for the buffets provided for guests, she was helping take care of Emma, Kelsey's five-year-old daughter. From the tidbits of information he'd gleaned from Lexi, Casey's other sister, Fred visited her garden early every morning to pick vegetables.

The garden and chicken coop were located near the bordering forest, so Jake took the path leading to the rear of the lodge. Before he reached the end of the building, he heard Fred's voice and froze. What Fred was saying would have sounded muffled to most humans, but because of his bear, he had exceptional hearing and could make out every word.

"Shoo, you can't be out here. It's not safe." Jake worried that her warning had been to another male. The jealousy tearing through his system disappeared the instant he heard her say, "Something might eat you."

Since she obviously wasn't conversing with a male, Jake was curious to see who she was having a conversation with. "Hey, Fred. Who are you talking to?" he asked as he rounded the corner and found her standing in the middle of the garden. Other than the rooster and two chickens moving between the rows of green plants, Fred was alone.

Jake realized too late that he should have done a better job announcing his presence. The birds squawked and flapped their wings, their short legs lifting off the ground as they hurried to get away from him. Fred had her back to him and must not have sensed his presence. She squeaked, then spun around and launched the tomato she'd been holding.

She had a good aim and a strong throw for a petite thing. The tomato hit Jake beneath his left shoulder, splitting upon impact, the juices seeping into the fabric of his shirt before it dropped to the ground.

Fred's cheeks flushed, and green eyes widened. "Oh my gosh, Jake." She gracefully jumped over plants as she rushed toward him. "I'm so sorry. Are you okay?" She reached for him and attempted to wipe away the parts of the tomato that remained on his shirt with her pink garden gloves.

"I'm all right. It's my fault for scaring you," Jake said as he wrapped his fingers around her bare wrist. The jolt that passed between them the instant their skin touched was warm. A tingle began at his fingertips and spread through his entire body, confirming that Fred was definitely his mate.

She must have been feeling the same thing, but instead of acting pleased, she gasped and yanked her hand from his grasp, her concern for his shirt no longer an issue. "What are you doing out here?"

Confused by her reaction, Jake furrowed his brows. Had Fred known from the first day they'd met that they were mates? Had she been disappointed, and was that why she'd been avoiding him? Jake preferred to deal with problems in a straightforward manner and worried that confronting her with his suspicions might not be the right way to handle the situation. "I, uh, live here." He'd opted to use a subtle approach and said the first thing he could think of, which sounded smug after hearing the words out loud.

Jake slipped his hands in the front pockets of his jeans. He noted the way her irritated gaze followed his motion. Her eyes immediately snapped back to his face as if she'd been caught admiring. Her face flushed, causing the freckles running along the bridge of her nose and cheeks that he'd always found adorable to darken. Maybe he'd been wrong about Fred being disappointed that he was her mate.

She shook her head. "No, I meant why are you doing sneaking around out here? You're never up this early in the morning."

His heart raced, and his stomach tightened. There was no way Fred could have known about his sleeping habits unless she'd been monitoring his activities. "How did you know I liked to sleep in?"

"I assumed since you never show up for coffee like everyone else," Fred said as she walked over and grabbed the basket she used to carry the vegetables she gathered.

When Fred finally turned around to face him, she fidgeted with the basket's handle and appeared as if she was waiting for him to say something.

Since he'd been a teenager, charming females had never been a problem. Now that they were alone, he found it difficult to talk to her about their connection or tell her that he thought she was the most interesting and beautiful female on the planet. Or that he thought her cooking was the best he'd ever eaten, even better than his mother's, and she excelled in the culinary arts.

Jake would've gladly discussed the contents in her basket if it meant spending more time with her. It was too bad that he and his bear were meat-eaters, and he'd never taken the time to learn about the different plants growing in her garden. The only reason he knew about tomatoes was because he liked to put them on his hamburgers.

Several sharp pokes to the back of Jake's leg put an end to finding a topic that didn't involve anything personal. "What the…" He sidestepped, doing his best to avoid trampling any plants and glared down at the rooster who'd decided to use him for pecking practice.

"It seems Grainger didn't appreciate being scared either," Fred said with a smirk.

Jake wanted to tell Fred the bird was lucky he didn't

pull out some of his feathers but refrained because it would most likely upset her and not help his cause. The chickens were part of Lexi's rescue menagerie, and all the females cared for them. The fact that the rooster had a name meant he was officially an adopted member of the family.

"I need to go and start breakfast for the guests," Fred said. "Since you're not doing anything important, would you mind unruffling the chickens' feathers and getting them back to the coop?" Her question sounded more like a directive, one he was certain required following.

Without giving him a chance to respond, Fred swept past him, purposely avoiding any contact with him or the rooster. Jake watched as she hurried toward the lodge, his gaze focused on her firm backside and swaying hips. Any time spent watching Fred always had the same effect on his body. More specifically, the front of his pants, which were now tight and uncomfortable.

When he heard the door on the side of the building close, he groaned and added another check mark to his list of failed attempts. He glanced at the bird, who was now pecking at something in the dirt, and said, "That could've gone better."

CHAPTER TWO

"Annoying," Fred said as she punched the mound of bread dough spread out before her on the counter. "Egotistical." Down came her fist again. "Frustrating," she growled, then smacked the mound harder. "Male." Her fist connected with the white gooey glob several more times, making it even flatter. At the rate she was going, she'd either run out of adjectives to describe Jake or flatten the dough to the thickness of a tortilla.

It was early, and members of the Walker family hadn't arrived yet, but Fred's uninterrupted moment of irritated contemplation wouldn't last long. The more she thought about Jake, the more she wished she'd hit him in the head with the tomato and not in the chest. She hated how a single word or even a glance from the infuriating male always sent heat rushing to her female parts.

Fred had known he was her mate and had suspected as much from the moment she'd met him. He had to know as well but hadn't said a word about it or done anything to acknowledge their connection. A connection that was confirmed the instant he wrapped his hand around her wrist, and an electrical tingle touched every nerve on her body. She could still feel the aftereffects which made her irritation worse.

So much for her plans to avoid him. Fred had convinced herself that when Jake learned about certain things from her past, he wouldn't want anything to do with her. Now that the mating bond had been fully awakened, ignoring Jake was going to be a lot harder. And deep down, a part of her didn't want to stay away from him, which would explain her irrational behavior.

Her fox thought Jake was wonderful and was angry when Fred had left him to take care of the chickens. The animal had been grumbling ever since and was getting harder to ignore. She didn't want to hear that things were complicated. As far as the silly creature was concerned, Fred should be spending more time with Jake, not trying to avoid him.

Mates were supposed to be a person's perfect match, the one they were meant to spend the rest of their life with. Jake was smart, handsome, and exuded a natural charm. Fred was certain he could have any female he chose. Was it possible he hadn't said anything because he was disappointed with the match and didn't want to hurt her feelings?

Maybe he didn't like her appearance. Maybe the fact that he easily towered over her by at least a foot bothered him. Or maybe he didn't like the color of her hair. Her bright crimson locks were her natural color, a gift from her fox.

Maybe he didn't like females who had freckles. She had plenty of them running along her cheeks and on other parts of her body. When she was younger, some of the children in the neighborhood teased her about them incessantly.

She didn't know why she let what Jake may or may not think bother her so much. Fred liked her independence and knew she shouldn't let what other people thought get to her. Who the heck needed a male anyway? Even if the brawny bear had firmly packed muscles and the most amazing dimples when he smiled. She'd been doing fine on her own before he'd showed up as a guest at the ranch. And she'd continue to do so even if fate had decided that they were supposed to be together when clearly Jake didn't support the idea.

Apparently, none of that mattered to her fox. The animal was snarling and urging Fred to claim Jake anyway. "Not. Going. To. Happen." She punched the dough with each word.

She'd have to do a better job of staying away from him. With any luck, he'd grow tired of annoying her and go back to Alaska. Fred wasn't about to admit that the notion of Jake leaving bothered her a lot or that it was the last thing she truly wanted.

She'd spent too many nights losing sleep and fantasizing about what it would be like to see him without any clothes and have him ask her to share his bed. Not that she had a problem dragging him into hers. It was one of the few things she and her fox agreed on when it came to Jake. Even now, the animal wanted nothing more than to curl up on his broad shoulders and press her muzzle against his neck.

"What's not gonna happen, Fred?" Emma asked, her pigtails swishing back and forth as she skipped into the kitchen.

"Um." Having the child arrive in time to hear Fred's rant and see her deliver another angry punch wasn't one of her better moments.

Emma climbed up on one of the stools on the opposite side of the center island and wrinkled her cute little nose. "Why are you mad at the dough?"

Kelsey, Lexi, and Casey strolled into the room right behind her. The sisters might have similar heights and facial features but were different when it came to personalities. Casey was the oldest and most responsible of the three. Kelsey, Emma's mother, was next in line, followed by Lexi, who possessed the least control when speaking her mind.

Since ranch life didn't require professional attire, they were all dressed in shirts, jeans, and boots. Emma had received a pair of cowboy boots for her last birthday and wore them with everything, including today's pair of short overalls.

"That's a darned good question," Casey said, walking to the counter behind Fred to grab a mug and pour herself some coffee. She glanced over her shoulder at her sisters. "Anyone else want a cup?" After receiving a yes from her sisters, she topped off two additional cups.

"The way you're assaulting that dough wouldn't have anything to do with a certain hottie with cute dimples, would it?" Lexi asked.

The growl was out before Fred could stop herself or slap a flour-covered hand over her mouth.

"I'll take that as a yes," Lexi said, taking a cup from Casey, then plopping on the stool next to Emma.

"Lexi," Kelsey warned with a glance at her daughter.

Emma rolled her dark eyes and huffed, "Mom, I know what dimples are 'cause I have them." She grinned and touched her cheeks. "But what does hottie mean?"

Casey choked on the coffee she'd just swallowed.

"Yeah, Kels." Lexi shifted sideways to smile at her sister.

Fred gave the counter a quick glance to ensure there weren't any objects, pieces of fruit, or freshly baked goods that the sisters could use as weapons. They were notorious for tossing things at one another, which almost always happened to be something she'd prepared for guests. The last food fight they'd had involved Fred's muffins, and poor Braden had taken one in the chest. Fortunately, he'd been a good sport about it.

Fred admired how well Kelsey handled being a single parent. Not to mention her restraint when dealing with her youngest sister. After a few seconds of glaring at her cup, Kelsey smiled at Emma and said, "It's another word for handsome."

"Oh," Emma drew out the word. "So, if Fred is talking to the dough, does that mean she likes Uncle Jake?"

"No, I…" Fred paused when the stares she received from the three females were laced with disbelief. Apparently, she wasn't fooling anyone, not even Emma, who was way more perceptive than most of the adults living on the property.

It was embarrassing to find out Fred's friends knew about Jake, but she shouldn't have been surprised by the sisters' assumptions. They might not be able to transform into animals because of their human mother, but they'd inherited some enhanced senses from their wolf-mshifter father. Abilities that allowed them to distinguish humans from shifters. They'd even gotten good at picking out the animals of others, something a full-blooded shifter could do easily. Sensing a mating bond didn't seem unreasonable.

If the females knew, then there was a good chance Braden did as well. He and Jake were closer than most brothers. Had Jake talked to his cousin about what he had yet to discuss with her?

If Braden was aware of her connection to Jake, he'd at least been nice enough to keep the information to himself rather than say anything to her. Though, with Casey being his mate, he'd probably discussed it with her. No doubt Noah knew as well, which upset Fred even more.

This was all Jake's fault, and if he'd been around, Fred would be taking her frustration out on him instead of the poor mound of dough. "Don't you guys have some stalls to clean, maybe a guest to help, or something, anything, to do somewhere else?"

Fred's next punch caused Emma to giggle so hard she would've fallen off her stool if Kelsey hadn't slid into the seat next to her.

"I'm good," Kelsey said. "How about you guys?"

"I don't have anywhere I need to be right now. Though I'd love to hear all the reasons why you don't like Jake,"

Lexi said.

"Me too," Casey said, reaching for the coffee pot so she could top off her cup.

Fred threw her hands in the air. "Fine, you win. I kind of like him…a little."

"Are you sure it's only a little?" Kelsey asked, her gaze dropping to the indented dough.

"Maybe. I don't know. He's just…"

"Hotter than hot." Lexi wiggled her brows.

Yes, Jake was an Adonis as far as looks went, but she wasn't about to tell her friends she wasn't disappointed by his appearance in the least. Nor was she going to mention how much she'd like to run her hands along the muscles of his broad chest or test to see if his chestnut strands were as silky as they looked.

She also wasn't going to share her thoughts about his kissable lips and how she knew they'd melt her from the inside out if she ever got a chance to taste them. Nope, Fred would be darned if she'd admit any of that out loud, no matter how much they pestered her.

Fred shrugged off Lexi's comment with a smirk. "I was thinking arrogant, stubborn, and infuriating." Afraid the dough would never rise if she didn't leave it alone, Fred molded it into a ball and placed it in a bowl.

"I'm glad to hear you're not holding back on how you feel," Casey laughed. "But are you certain you didn't leave anything out?"

Fred pinned her friend with a narrow-eyed glare.

Lexi propped her elbows on the counter and rested her chin on her hands. "Now that we know you like him a lot, what seems to be the problem?"

Fred adored these females. They'd never pressured her to be anything she wasn't or to tell them about her past. Her uncle Miles might be the only living relative she had left, but the sisters treated her more like family than he ever had. Thinking about the male and why she'd left home nearly eight months ago didn't help the stress she was experiencing.

Fred also knew if she told them what was going on with Jake, they'd want to help. Maybe even discuss the situation with Jake and convince him to talk to her.

For any other problem, she'd welcome their interference, but not this time. Deep down, she wanted, no needed, Jake to figure things out on his own. Either claim her or tell her he didn't want her. And if it was the latter, she needed Jake to leave and go back to Alaska. Because seeing him every day and knowing they would never be together meant she'd have to give up her home forever. "I don't want to talk about it."

Thankfully, the sound of heavy footsteps echoing from the outside hallway and heading in their direction prevented any more questions. Fred spent the next few seconds holding her breath and secretly hoping that Jake had decided to come looking for her.

She forced back a dejected groan when a male she didn't recognize appeared in the kitchen doorway. Wearing tight jeans and a T-shirt that flaunted his muscular build, he sauntered into the room with a confident swagger. "Excuse me, can one of you help me?" he asked, flashing a cocky smile as if he expected every female he encountered to find him charming and appealing.

Too bad for him that these particular females had no use for a male like him, Fred included. "I stopped at the registration desk, but there wasn't anyone there."

Kelsey slid off her stool. "I'm sorry, did you have a reservation?"

As far as Fred knew, all the guests scheduled to stay the week had arrived via bus and been picked up from Waynesrock the day before.

"No, it was a last-minute decision on my part," he said. "I was in the area, so I thought I'd stop by and see if you still had a cabin available."

Nobody was ever just in the neighborhood. The ranch was quite a ways from town, and anyone who searched for it had to get off a two-lane highway to find it.

Fred wasn't the only one who found his explanation a little strange. Lexi and Casey were no longer smiling. Emma had gotten down from her stool, was clutching her mother's leg, and warily eying the male.

"I'm Kelsey Walker, one of the owners. And these are my sisters, Casey and Lexi." She swept her arm through the air. "My daughter, Emma." She placed a protective hand on the child's head. "And our cook, Fred."

The male jerked his head in Fred's direction, his inquisitive gaze making her uneasy. "Fred, that's a unique name. Is it short for something?"

Fred wasn't about to tell a complete stranger that her full name, one she hadn't used since she was a child, was Frederica. "Yes," she answered, biting back her usual flippant response of telling him it was none of his business.

Kelsey, sensing everyone's tension, stepped into her professional business mode. She picked up Emma and handed her to Lexi. "I'll be right back, okay?" After receiving a nod from her daughter, she faced the male. "I'm sorry, I forgot to ask your name."

"Conrad Morgan. It's nice to meet you all," he said, smugly grinning as if he hadn't noticed that his arrival had put all the females in the room on edge.

"Why don't you come with me, and I'll see what we have available?" Kelsey asked, motioning him from the room.

"That would be great, thanks," Conrad said, giving Fred one more scrutinizing look over his shoulder before leaving the room.

Lexi tightened her grip on Emma when she squirmed to get off her lap and go after her mom. "Hey, little one, why don't we stay here and help Fred?"

Besides being an arrogant male, Conrad hadn't done anything to make Fred believe he was a threat, yet his departure didn't ease her discomfort, nor did the idea of

Kelsey being alone with him. Seeing the scowls on Casey's and Lexi's faces, she was sure they didn't either.

Luckily, the area used for check-ins which contained a computer and all the guest information was located at the end of the same hallway the stranger had used to reach the kitchen. The room wasn't far away. If Kelsey needed help, all she had to do was call out and they'd hear her.

Her fox wasn't happy about the male's presence either. She was very protective of the Walker family, refusing to stop pacing and snarling until Conrad left the room. Fred had been concerned by Emma's reaction to the male and was glad when she finally relaxed her grip on Lexi's shirt. Fred had never met Emma's father but assumed he'd been human. After noting the child's behavior, Fred wondered if she'd inherited some shifter senses through her mother's bloodline.

Lexi kept Emma on her lap and swiveled on the stool once the sound of footsteps in the hallway disappeared. "Did you see the way that guy was checking you out?" she asked Fred.

"Lexi," Casey scolded, then glanced at Emma and touched her ear, a reminder that their niece didn't need to hear whatever her sister was about to say next.

"All I'm saying is that it looks like Uncle Jake better get with the program, or Mr. Hottie Wolf out there might swoop in and steal Fred away from him."

"Oh, yeah, that's so much better," Casey said sarcastically.

"What do you say we go find Jake and warn him that he's got some competition?" Lexi tapped the tip of Emma's nose, then lifted her off her lap so she could slide to the floor.

Ready to throttle Lexi, Fred ignored her own rules about no food fights in the kitchen and reached for the first thing she could find, which happened to be some green onions she'd picked earlier. "Lexi," she growled, wiggling the bulbed ends at her friend.

"Time to go." Lexi scooped up a giggling Emma and hurried through the entryway and into the hallway.

"Don't worry, it's going to be okay," Casey said, though she didn't sound very convincing when she placed a comforting hand on Fred's shoulder. "She was most likely kidding, and they're on their way out to the barn to feed the animals."

With Lexi, there were times when it was hard to tell if she was being serious or teasing. In this case, Fred hoped Casey was right. If Jake ever got around to making his intentions known, she wanted it to be his idea, not because someone else had prodded him into it.

"Is it me, or do you think it's a little strange that someone would show up all the way out here without a reservation?" Casey stared at the empty doorway a little longer as if contemplating something else.

"I was thinking the same thing," Fred said, gaining Casey's full attention.

"Do you think he's working for Harlan?" Casey asked.

Harlan Sawyer was the owner of the Wolf's Claw Ranch and their biggest competitor. His place housed a variety of sifters, not just wolves. Of course, the males working there didn't have a healthy respect for the law. They'd caused plenty of problems for Casey and her sisters in the past.

Harlan wanted to purchase the Crescent Canyon and add it to his own. At one point, he'd resorted to sabotage in order to get it. Before Braden and Jake had arrived, the ranch had been in financial trouble, and Fred had been concerned that the wolf might actually succeed.

Harlan also had a thing for Casey, and his pursuit had finally ended in a battle between his wolf and Braden's bear. A fight that Harlan lost. Braden had warned him to stay away from the ranch and his mate, but it was hard to know if Harlan would heed his threats.

"I have no idea," Fred said.

Now that things were turning around, Fred hoped they

wouldn't have to deal with Harlan anymore.

If Braden got drawn into another fight, Jake would support him. Fred felt sure they could both handle themselves, even against terrible odds, but the thought of Jake being hurt in any way had her twisting the hem of her apron.

"I don't want to say anything to Lexi and Kelsey yet, not until we know for sure why Conrad is really here," Casey said. "I do think I need to tell Braden and Jake, maybe even Noah, so they can help keep an eye on him."

"Not a bad idea," Fred said, then another thought occurred to her, one equally disturbing because it involved her. "What if Conrad's working for my uncle?"

Casey was the only one on the ranch who knew about Fred's past and her reasons for remaining in seclusion. The sisters didn't usually keep secrets from each other, at least not when it came to important matters that could affect everyone's lives. When Fred had first told Casey about her uncle's attempt to force her into an unwanted marriage, they'd both agreed that it wasn't something they needed to concern her sisters with.

Kelsey was having a tough time raising a child alone because Emma's father was a jerk and had dumped her after learning she was pregnant. And Lexi was...Lexi. Since she struggled with filtering her thoughts, they'd been afraid she might inadvertently share the information with the wrong person.

Fred would hate to give up her home, but if she caught the slightest glimmer that her uncle had sent Conrad to take her back to the miserable life he had planned for her, she wouldn't hesitate to leave the ranch and find a new place to live or hide.

"Do you think he'd send someone to look for you after all this time?" Casey asked. "Or that they'd be able to trace you here?"

Fred cringed and said, "I hope not, but Miles is a conniving, greedy male who doesn't give up easily." She'd learned the hard way that underestimating her uncle was a mistake. One she never planned to make again.

She hadn't left a trail of any kind, only paying with cash and using a false name wherever she stayed. Money didn't last forever, and the occasional odd job hadn't done much to replenish the funds she'd taken from her savings account before leaving home. Finding the cook's position at the ranch had been a miraculous answer to her situation, one she couldn't pass up, which was why she desperately hoped she was wrong about Conrad.

Panicked by the thought of Jake finding out brought on a bought of nausea. Fred placed a hand on Casey's arm. "I understand needing to tell Jake about Conrad possibly working for Harlan, but promise me you won't say anything to him about my uncle."

Casey frowned. "Why not? He's your mate."

"What makes you say that?" Fred asked a little too defensively.

"Please," Casey said, shaking her head. "Anyone who's spent more than five minutes in the same room with you two can tell."

"Does that mean everyone knows?" Fred groaned, her earlier suspicions confirmed.

"Everyone except maybe Emma, but knowing Lexi…"

"Then Emma knows too." Fred slumped against the counter and sighed. "You still can't tell Jake."

Casey placed her hands on her hips. She didn't have to say anything because the glare she leveled at Fred was enough to extract an explanation. "We haven't exactly discussed the situation, and I don't want him to be overprotective because he thinks it's the right thing to do, not because he actually cares."

"I'm pretty sure he does care," Casey said, holding up her hand before Fred could argue. "But for now, I'll honor your wishes and only speak to Braden about it."

"I know I'm asking a lot, but can you make Braden promise not to tell Jake either?" Fred asked, then, to ensure he didn't get the information from another source, she added, "That goes for Kelsey and Lexi too. When and if the time comes, I'd like to be the one to tell them."

"As long as Conrad doesn't pose a threat, no one else will hear about it." Casey pulled Fred into a tight hug, then took a step back but didn't release her. "And if you're thinking about taking off...don't. You're family. We protect our own, and I'd rather not have to waste my time tracking you down and dragging you back here."

CHAPTER THREE

After Jake's unsuccessful attempt to discuss his connection with Fred and the possibility of exploring any kind of relationship, he'd planned to head back to his room in the employees' bunkhouse to change, but Whiskey Belle, the friendliest horse on the place, had whinnied at him as he walked past the corral. He grabbed a treat from the bin inside the barn, then stopped to rub her nose.

Casey told him she always found it therapeutic to talk to the sweet-natured mare. Jake wasn't sure how helpful talking to the animal would be but thought he'd give it a try anyway. "Belle, you're a female, right?" She snorted on his palm as she snatched the treat he held out for her.

"Of course, you are. Thanks for pointing it out. I've recently found my mate and—"

"Hey, Jake, I'm surprised to see you up this early," Braden said as he strolled up next to him, then leaned against the fence with his arms braced along the top rail. "Is everything okay?"

"I had something to do." Jake continued to rub Belle's nose.

"You still haven't told her, have you? Is that why you're asking the horse for advice?"

Jake grunted, uninterested in answering or receiving a lecture. It was embarrassing enough to be caught discussing his personal life with Belle, but having his cousin remind him of the situation with Fred made it worse. They'd had the same talk several times since Braden and Casey's wedding. Speaking to females had never been a problem for Jake, but it was different with Fred. She was his mate, the one and only relationship that would ever matter, and the last thing he wanted to do was screw things up.

Now that Jake was pretty sure Fred was aware that they were mates, especially after the tingling jolt they'd shared earlier, he was still trying to figure out why she hadn't said anything either. The longer they went without talking about it, the more he worried that she might be disappointed with him. He knew they were supposed to be perfectly matched, but what if there was something about his appearance or personality that she didn't like.

They hadn't been around each other long enough for her to get to know him as a person. And she never would unless they spent more time together, preferably without anyone else around.

As far as he was concerned, there wasn't anything he'd seen regarding Fred that he didn't like. Even keeping her hair pulled back in a ponytail and wearing clothes that concealed her femininity was endearing and suited her.

Jake had yet to make eye contact with Braden, so his cousin leaned forward to see his face and got a glimpse of his shirt. After a quick sniff, Braden asked, "What happened to your shirt? Why do you look and smell like you've been rolling around in a tomato patch?" His cousin took another sniff, then chuckled. No doubt picking up Fred's scent as well. "You didn't by any chance tangle with a certain female cook who can shift into a fox, did you?"

Jake gripped the top board of the fence tighter and answered his cousin with a sidelong glare.

Braden scratched his chin, a sure sign he wasn't willing

to drop the subject. "Have you thought about talking to the girls? I'll bet they'd be happy to tell you what you're doing wrong."

By girls, Jake knew Braden was referring to Casey, Lexi, and Kelsey. He pressed his lips together and forced back his bear's growl.

Braden smirked. "Heck, Emma could probably give you some decent pointers."

"Great, I can't believe you're suggesting I take mating advice from a five-year-old." If there weren't guests around, Jake would've enjoyed shoving Braden's face in the nearest pile of horse manure. He thought about their plans to add fake shifter fights to the activities and how now would be a great time to get in some practice.

If shifting didn't include shredding his clothes and ruining the new boots he'd bought for horseback riding, Jake would definitely consider letting out his bear so he could give his cousin a few good swipes. It might upset Casey, but Jake was confident he could convince her that her mate deserved the scrapes and bruises he'd receive if they tussled.

Braden shrugged. "Just trying to help."

"And you wonder why I'm talking to the horse. At least Belle doesn't go out of her way to ridicule me." Jake hadn't meant to sound so snarly, but he couldn't help himself.

"Sorry, cuz." Braden must have realized he'd gone too far. The empathy lacing his cousin's tone should have made Jake feel better, but it only made him feel worse. Braden clamped a hand on Jake's shoulder. "Why don't you take a ride into town with me? I need to pick up some supplies for Casey."

"What about the trail ride?" Jake was a ranch employee, and one of his main jobs was helping Kelsey get the horses ready and going along on the rides for the guests. He took pride in his work, whatever task he was assigned, and didn't like dumping his responsibilities on someone else.

"I'm sure Noah won't mind helping her today," Braden

said. Noah was a wolf shifter and a couple of years older than Jake. He'd worked for the Walker family since he'd been a teen. Jake liked the male and hated giving him extra work.

"Maybe some time away from the ranch will help you put things into perspective," Braden said. "It'll give you a chance to come up with a better game plan."

Jake was glad Braden hadn't pointed out that his current way of doing things wasn't working.

The dilemma with Fred was all he could think about, and he decided to heed Braden's advice. "You might be right. A change of scenery couldn't hurt." He wasn't confident that being away from Fred was the best idea, not when his bear was growling and warning him not to leave her. The animal didn't understand, nor did he care about the human technicalities that went along with courting a mate. All his bear cared about was making Fred theirs, something the surly creature thought should have happened weeks ago.

The ranch was in a remote location, and all their guests that week were couples, some of them shifters. Jake didn't have to worry about any unattached males trying to gain her attention, so he didn't think anything would happen to Fred if he spent a few hours away from the place.

CHAPTER FOUR

Jake and Braden hadn't said much to one another during the long drive into Waynesrock. The great thing about growing up together and being close was understanding each other's needs. Riding in silence wasn't uncomfortable because neither of them required the other to pass the time in conversation. The trip hadn't resolved his troubling issues, but it had given Jake a chance to relax and develop a few ideas about dealing with Fred.

Once they'd arrived in town, Jake continued to stare out the passenger door window expecting Braden to turn into the mercantile's lot, not drive past it. He shifted to face his cousin and said, "I thought we came here to get supplies."

"Actually, I might have exaggerated that part a little bit," Braden said, glancing at Jake, then focusing back on the road.

"Exactly how much is a little?" The last time Jake had heard similar words, they'd stopped at the town's only jewelry store to get an engagement ring for Casey. Since they were now happily mated, Jake couldn't think of any other reason for his cousin to be driving to the other end of town.

"Um…all of it," Braden said sheepishly.

It irked Jake that Braden had misled him, but giving him a chance to explain was the right thing to do. There would be plenty of time afterward to handle things bear to bear if he didn't like what his cousin had to say. "Are you going to tell me where we *are* going and why you couldn't tell me before we left?"

"I didn't think you'd get in the truck if I told you the truth." Braden rubbed the back of his head. "But in my defense, I was sworn to secrecy."

Secret or not, Jake wanted answers. "Braden," he growled, letting his bear seep into his voice.

"Just so you know, I told her she should've called you first. I knew you weren't going to be happy if she showed up unannounced."

It didn't take long for Jake to figure out that the 'she' his cousin referred to had to be his mother. He gripped the door's armrest, barely managing to keep his claws from extending beyond his fingertips. "Are you saying my mother is here…now?"

"Not only your mom," Braden said. "She brought mine too." He didn't sound entirely thrilled about the upcoming visit either.

Why would Braden care if his mother showed up? His cousin had it easy. Aunt Violet was going to love Casey. On the other hand, Jake's life was about to become a lot more complicated. He knew his mother would adore Fred, but he could already hear the lecture he was going receive when she found out they hadn't discussed being mates yet. Those questions would lead to others that involved claiming and future grandchildren. Without any decent answers, Jake didn't want to think about what would happen after that.

"Does Casey know?"

"Yeah, but if it helps, we didn't find out they were coming until yesterday," Braden said.

"Not really, but there's nothing we can do about it

now." Jake might be angry and feel somewhat betrayed that he hadn't received a heads up, but he couldn't blame Braden for not telling him, not if his mother had manipulated him into a promise.

He remembered how excited his mother and aunt were when they'd learned about the trip Braden and he were taking to Wyoming and why. Thinking about mates made Jake's chest tighten, and he asked, "You didn't tell them about Fred, did you?"

Jake could always trust his cousin when it came to tough situations. Having a mate was new territory for both of them, and he hoped it hadn't changed anything.

"Of course not," Braden huffed. "But the minute she sees the two of you in the same room, she'll be able to figure it out for herself. They both will."

"That's what I'm afraid of," Jake said, scrubbing his hand along his face. He and Braden had been suffering from their matchmaking attempts for years. When his mother and aunt got together, they were notorious busybodies, and there was no way to predict what they would do next. The problem was, they weren't satisfied with meddling in their offspring's lives. Oh, no, all their male friends had to endure what both females referred to as some neighborly help.

Their kind of assistance could make things with Fred worse. What if it ruined everything, and she decided not to have anything to do with him? The thought of losing Fred before he got a chance to make things right had him reaching for the door handle.

Jake could see the large sign for the bus station looming in the distance. "Stop the truck and let me out." Maybe if he jumped out now, he could transform into his bear and reach the ranch before Braden and his female relatives did. At least he'd be able to warn Fred before his mother talked to her. Too bad Braden was faster and engaged the automatic locks before he could open the door.

"I'm not stopping the truck," Braden said with a hint of a grin.

Jake shot an incredulous look at his cousin, irritated that he found the situation amusing. "This is your aunt we're talking about. The one who cuffs the back of our heads to make a point." Child-rearing in the shifter world was different than in the human world, and they'd both earned enough smacks over the years to cause bald spots, which luckily, being part bear prevented from happening.

Braden had earned more than Jake because his mother tended to be overprotective when it came to her son, especially if they got caught doing something they shouldn't.

"I don't think it's going to be as bad as you think," Braden said, flipping the signal indicator, then slowing the vehicle to turn into the bus parking lot. There weren't any airports close by, and unless a person rented a car and planned to drive for several hours, taking a bus was the only way to get to Waynesrock.

The pressure in his chest increased, and Jake wondered how upset Casey would be if she had to replace the entire door of the truck. If he shifted inside the cab, he could easily rip the metal off its hinges and most likely cause Braden to wreck. Neither option was acceptable, so he remained seated and waited for his cousin to park and disengage the door's lock before he could get out.

Visitor parking was along one side of the building, so they had to walk around to the front to find their mothers. The females were sitting on a bench underneath an awning, chatting with several other people who were waiting for the next bus or expecting rides.

"Mom, Aunt Violet," Jake said, shuffling his feet as he walked toward them. "What a nice surprise." He tried hard to sound like he meant it but was afraid his lack of enthusiasm had leaked out in his voice. Any other time, he'd be excited to see his mother, but her anticipated reaction when she heard about the situation with Fred was something he could do without.

Celia was the eldest of the two sisters. Other than a few silver strands hinting that the females were older, it always amazed Jake that they appeared at least ten years younger than their actual ages. They both stayed in shape and dressed fashionably, usually wearing nice shirts and casual pants, enhancing their youthful appearance.

"Jake," Celia squealed, jumping up from the bench and wrapping her arms around his neck in a tight squeeze. "It's so good to see you." Once she released him, she ran her hands along his arms, then eyed the length of him. "It looks like Wyoming is agreeing with you." She glanced at Braden. "Actually, both of you."

"Hey, Aunt Celia," Braden said, reaching for Jake's mom after he'd finished giving his mother a hug.

Violet wasn't as vocal as her sister, but she did pull Jake into her arms, then patted his cheek and smiled.

"How long are you planning to stay?" Jake said before she could chastise him about not calling more often or question him about what he'd been doing and if he'd found his mate yet. Wishing her stay only lasted a couple of days was too much to hope for. His mother could make a lot of things happen in a short period of time, so it was always a good idea to know what he'd be dealing with.

"We've missed you boys something terrible," Celia said, giving Violet a conspiratorial glance before answering. "We've decided to stay at least a week."

"Maybe longer if we're having a good time," Violet said.

"That's great, isn't it, Jake?" Braden asked as he nudged his shoulder.

"Yeah, sure," Jake said, wondering if Casey's aunt Trudy would have a problem letting him stay with her if he showed up on the doorstep of her secluded cabin in the mountains.

"Since you appear to be all right,"—Celia raised her brow—"I assume the reason you haven't called for the last two weeks is because you found your mate and have been spending all of your time working on my future grandbabies."

Jake could feel the heat rising along his neck and cheeks even before his mother reached for the collar of his shirt and pulled it away so she could inspect the skin beneath it. "Though, I don't see a claiming mark." She took a step back, crossing her arms, and narrowing her dark eyes.

The female was incorrigible, and Jake hated it when she treated him like he was still in high school. "Really, mom," he said, taking a step back and readjusting his shirt. He couldn't believe she was discussing his nonexistent love life. It was bad enough when she did it around family but doing it in front of a group of strangers was unacceptable. It was impossible for the people waiting to have their luggage loaded on the bus to avoid overhearing their conversation. And for any shifters in the group, the words were much clearer and not prone to misinterpretation.

They'd caught the attention of a female wolf shifter who appeared to be around the same age as Celia and Violet. She didn't bother hiding the grin that suggested she agreed with his mother.

"Speaking of grandchildren…" When Violet turned her attention on Braden, Celia's interest perked as well.

Braden held up his hand and scowled. "I want you to promise me right now that you're not going to pressure Casey about children." After a second, he added, "Or me either."

Personally, Jake would've been happy if Violet continued. At least he'd no longer be under his mother's scrutiny.

"What makes you think I'd ever do such a thing?" Violet asked.

Braden crossed his arms and glared at his mother. "I mean it, mom."

"Fine," she harrumphed and rolled her eyes. Braden

didn't seem satisfied with her response and started tapping his booted foot.

"Oh, for goodness sake," Violet snarled and threw her hands in the air. "I promise."

"Thanks," Braden grinned and kissed her cheek, which immediately blossomed into a bright red.

"That goes for you too," Jake said to Celia, though he was certain she'd never follow his directive.

Celia stubbornly jutted out her chin. "I'm not agreeing to anything until after I've met your mate."

Jake swallowed hard, knowing that withholding the truth would be impossible. "About that…"

"Don't tell me you've been down here all this time and haven't found her yet," Celia said.

Jake groaned. "I found her, but it's complicated."

"Mom, Aunt Celia," Braden said as he tucked his mother's makeup case under his beefy arm, then reached for her two remaining suitcases. "I know Casey is looking forward to meeting you, so why don't we get going and finish this conversation on the drive back?"

Jake gave his cousin an appreciative nod. "That sounds like a great idea." He placed his hand on his mother's shoulder, urging her to follow Braden while he retrieved her suitcases. If the disapproving backward glance he received from Celia was any indication, his reprieve wouldn't last long.

As soon as Braden exited the parking lot, Jake discovered he'd been right.

CHAPTER FIVE

Fred placed the last of the bowls, pans, and utensils she'd used to prepare lunch in the dishwasher and pressed the start button, satisfied when she heard a low drone as the machine came to life. She leaned against the counter and stared out the window at the lush forest and house situated behind the lodge.

Lately, it seemed all her spare moments were spent thinking about Jake, so she wasn't surprised when her thoughts drifted in his direction.

He might not want to acknowledge that they were mates, but since he'd arrived on the ranch, he'd never missed a meal. Fred didn't think being smacked with a tomato or having to deal with the chickens would keep him from showing up for lunch.

She would've gone looking for him if Casey hadn't mentioned that he'd gone into town with Braden. Fred justified the protective urge she was feeling by convincing herself it was because he was part of the ranch's extended family, not because the bond between them was growing stronger, and she wanted to be close to him. Her fox had strongly disagreed and made a noise that sounded a lot like a snort.

"Excuse me," an unfamiliar female voice said, startling Fred from her thoughts.

Irritated by the unexpected intrusion, Fred spun around, searching for a calming tone before saying, "Yes."

Guests rarely found their way back to the kitchen, and this was the second one to arrive today. Fred wondered if someone had taken down the sign posted in the hallway that read, "Ranch Employees Only" and planned to check when she left the lodge.

After the trouble they'd had with Harlan, she'd gotten in the habit of making sure anyone she encountered on the property was supposed to be there, which included any new guests.

Fred had never seen the female standing in the entryway before, but she had warm dark eyes and a smile that immediately put her at ease. Her shoulder-length hair was a light brown and sprinkled with silver strands. Oddly, her features seemed vaguely familiar, but Fred couldn't figure out why.

"Are you Fred?" the female asked.

"I am," she answered, trying to sound more curious than wary. "Who are you?"

"I'm Celia Parker. Jake's mom."

That explained why the female's features looked so familiar. "Oh," Fred stammered to keep from gasping. It only took a few seconds for her shock to be replaced with the frustrating desire to track down Jake and ask him why he'd neglected to tell her his mother was visiting, but that would involve discussing the topic they'd both been avoiding.

Even so, meeting a mate's parents was a big deal, and failing to warn her was wrong. If Jake was smart, he'd stay clear of her for the rest of the day, maybe even tomorrow. There was no guarantee that telling him what she thought wouldn't include her fury and perhaps a show of her fox's claws. Getting the animal to comply would be moot because the only kind of nibbling she was interested in involved nuzzling Jake's neck.

After taking a calming breath, Fred wiped her hands on her apron and stepped around the center island. "It's a pleasure to meet you."

"You as well," Celia said, ignoring Fred's offered hand and pulling her into a tight hug. Either the female was a natural hugger, or her enthusiasm stemmed from something else. Was it possible Celia knew she was Jake's mate, and if so, were things about to get awkward?

"I don't want to keep you from your work," Celia said as soon as she released Fred. "The bus drive was long, and Casey said you might have some tea available."

With the right motivation, most mothers loved to talk about their children. Maybe Fred could use Celia's visit to her advantage. "You're not keeping me from anything at the moment," Fred said, motioning toward the stools sitting near the island. "Please have a seat, and I'll get us some tea." She walked over to the cabinet and pulled out two glasses.

"Well, if you're sure it's not a problem," Celia said.

When Fred turned around, she noticed that Celia had already made herself comfortable and grinned. She had a feeling Jake's mother had her own agenda and wasn't going to leave even if Fred insisted.

After filling both glasses, she set one in front of Celia, then joined her. "So, tell me about your trip."

***

If Jake thought things might go in his favor once he'd returned to the ranch, or that the ever-tightening knot in his stomach would miraculously disappear, he'd been mistaken. With his mother's arrival, putting off the discussion with Fred about them being mates was no longer possible. Getting to her before one of his female relatives did was another issue and one that turned out to be extremely difficult.

After helping his mother and aunt settle into their guest cabin, he planned to find Fred while Braden introduced them to Casey. Only fate had other ideas. Darla, one of the rescue goats, had a habit of getting out of her pen, and Lexi needed Noah's help rounding her up. That meant Kelsey would have to put away the horses after the morning trail ride without any assistance.

Making sure the horses were well taken care of was one of Jake's jobs. He already felt guilty about having Noah cover for him so he could accompany Braden to town. There was no way he would let Kelsey handle the remainder of the tasks herself.

By the time he'd finished helping Kelsey, it was late afternoon. The evening meal was still several hours away, leaving plenty of time before Fred started her preparations. Jake was certain he'd find her working in the lodge and decided to start there first.

He bypassed the empty dining hall and headed for the corridor that led to the back of the building and the kitchen.

"Cinnamon, really?" Jake heard his mother's voice and froze. "I never would've thought to use that," she continued.

"I've found that a pinch makes all the difference," Fred said, her voice happy and stress-free as if she was genuinely enjoying the conversation.

Maybe he'd gotten lucky and arrived in time to prevent any damage from happening. Knowing how determined his mother could be, he strongly doubted it.

"Interesting, I'm going to try…" Celia paused, then said. "Jake, what have I told you about eavesdropping. Stop lurking in the hallway and join us."

Jake cringed, and his bear cowered. Celia had been scolding him as if he were a cub since he was little. When he still lived at home, which had been a few years now, sneaking in or out of the house without being caught had been impossible. He'd forgotten about her uncanny ability

35

to sense when he was close by and should've known better than to linger outside the room too long.

He knew his mother's overbearing behavior was done out of love, so he usually ignored it. Proving to Fred that he'd be a good mate was all that mattered. Now that Celia had embarrassed him in front of her, retreating was no longer an option.

"Hey, mom, Fred," Jake said as he walked into the room, his gaze locking with Fred's sparkling green eyes. Even more distracting was the way her scent, an enticing mixture of her unique smell combined with lavender from her body wash, blended with the aroma of baked foods that filled the air.

"I didn't want to interrupt," Jake said, forcing himself to look at his mother. "I wanted to see how you were settling in and ask if you needed any help unpacking."

Judging by their scowls, neither female believed his lame explanation. Jake held his breath, hoping that he wouldn't have to backpedal, especially if his mother asked him why he was looking for her in the kitchen instead of her cabin where the clothes were located.

Celia tsked and rolled her eyes. "I appreciate the offer, but I can unpack later. Besides, I was parched from the trip, and Casey told me to make myself at home, then pointed me in the direction of the kitchen." She smiled at Fred. "And I'm glad she did because Fred was nice enough to share some of her cooking secrets with me."

Clearly, the two females were on friendly terms, so had Jake been worrying for nothing? Was his mother actually going to abide by his wishes not to interfere? It would be a first, and he wasn't about to take any chances.

Casey didn't miss much and probably suspected that Fred was his mate, but it didn't mean she'd gone out of her way to make his life miserable. Sending Celia to Fred was most likely as innocent as it sounded and not part of a bigger plot to do some matchmaking.

"Jake," Fred said, cutting his musing short. Her voice

sounded calm and pleasant, but the accusatory glare in her eyes was hard to miss. "Why didn't you tell me your mother was coming for a visit? I would've changed my menu to make some of her favorites."

"I…" Jake stammered.

Celia reached across the counter and squeezed Fred's hand. "I'm afraid he didn't know," she said with all the innocence of an adoring mother. "Violet wanted to meet Casey, so I tagged along so I could surprise my sweet boy."

After all the chastising his mother had given him during the drive back to the ranch, he was shocked that she'd come to his rescue. Knowing his mother and her quest to ensure she'd be getting grandchildren, Jake was afraid she wouldn't leave until she saw a mating mark on Fred's beautiful shoulder, which could end up being months away. He and his bear were longing to see the mark themselves, but it was never going to happen if things kept going wrong.

Determined to move things in the right direction, yet wary of Celia's sudden change in tactics, Jake said, "I heard something about cinnamon and wondered if you were going to prepare some of your tasty dishes while you were here." He patted his stomach, hoping a little flattery might help distract her.

"I don't have any plans at the moment," Celia said. "Why?"

Jake didn't miss the underlying annoyance in her tone. It was subtle, a perfected skill that usually went unnoticed by others. "No reason." He narrowed his eyes, hoping she'd get the hint and leave so he could talk to Fred alone.

"Well, then, was there anything else you needed?" Celia asked, not budging from her seat.

"Not that I can think of."

"You're more than welcome to join us," Fred said, sharing a grin with Celia.

The friendly relationship the females had developed in

the short time they'd spent together was reminiscent of the closeness Celia and Violet shared when they were in the midst of causing trouble. Jake knew he wouldn't stand a chance if he stayed. Deciding that a hasty retreat might be best, he moved backward toward the doorway. "Um, maybe later."

CHAPTER SIX

Jake couldn't believe he'd officially become a stalker.

Up until recently, he never relied on luck or believed in fate. He'd been convinced the only way to succeed was by making things happen himself. But after today, he was seriously reconsidering his views. It seemed like no matter how hard he tried to get Fred alone so they could talk, someone or something else got in the way.

After leaving Fred and Celia alone with the hope that sharing cooking tips was the only topic they discussed, he'd found a place where he could watch the lodge without appearing conspicuous. His plan to wait for his mother to leave so he could finally talk to Fred didn't go as he'd anticipated. By the time Celia left the lodge, Casey and Lexi had arrived to help Fred with dinner preparations.

Normally, Jake would be one of the first people through the buffet line. His stomach had rumbled all the way to the lodge, but once he'd gotten inside and seen Fred setting out the metal food containers, the reminders of his day's failed attempts jabbed him in the gut, and he'd lost his appetite.

He scanned the room and spotted his mother and aunt sitting a few tables away from the buffet line, happily participating in a conversation with several other guests. He knew he should join them but wasn't in the mood to endure any more of their meddling.

Jake wasn't the type to mope or admit defeat, but in order to regroup and come up with a better plan, he needed to keep some distance from Fred so he could think clearly. He took a seat at one of the tables farthest from the buffet area that offered a clear view of the entire room.

It seemed that Jake hadn't picked a location secluded enough to keep his cousin from joining him. "Why are you sitting way over here?" Braden asked as he set his plate heaping with food on the table, then took a seat on the bench opposite Jake. "And why haven't you gotten any food? You aren't afraid she's going to bite, are you?" His added chuckle grated along Jake's already hypersensitive nerves.

"Are you talking about Fred or my mother?" Jake asked, pretending to ignore the underlying reference to shifter mating. He was seriously going to punch his cousin if his intent was to continue chastising him about the situation with Fred.

With all the tension rippling through his body, sparring with his cousin's bear had a lot of appeal. He wouldn't have thought twice about provoking his cousin into a brawl if they were back in Alaska. His bear was all for doing something that would impress his mate and was happy to oblige. Jake might not know Fred as well as he'd like, but he was sure she wouldn't appreciate a show of strength. Neither would his female relatives. He was already feeling the weight of his mother's disappointment and didn't need to add more items to the list.

"I could ask you the same thing since your mom is sitting on the other side of the room."

Braden winced. "Point taken," he said, then picked up a crispy fried chicken leg. "What happened to all that Parker charm? You've never had a problem with females before, so why are you having difficulty now?"

"Because being rejected wasn't a big deal, and neither was moving on." Since he and his bear hadn't connected with any of the females back home, he could deal with the occasional bruised ego from being turned down for a date. "This is Fred, my mate. I can't afford to screw it up."

"I'm afraid that might already be happening," Casey said as she took a seat on the bench next to Braden. "And if you don't do something to fix it soon, you might lose her altogether."

It was bad enough having to discuss his failures with his cousin, but having Casey chime in made it even worse. "How do you know?" Jake groaned. "Did she say something?" He hated sounding like a hormonal teenager, but he desperately wanted to know what he was dealing with since getting Fred alone seemed to be impossible.

"Not so much in words, but…" Casey paused, her gaze shooting to the area behind him.

Jake glanced over his shoulder and found Emma moving toward them. Even with her concerned expression, the child was adorable. Her hair was pulled up in pigtails, secured with little pink bows that matched the shirt underneath her short overalls. Her cowboy boots might clash with her outfit, but they were her favorites and the only thing she'd let anyone put on her feet.

For a child of five, she had the stealth of a panther. He kept forgetting that she liked to sneak into rooms and listen to the adults. Which sometimes could be a bad thing because she also had a habit of repeating what she heard at the most inopportune moments.

Jake also understood why Casey hadn't finished her statement. She must have thought what she had to say wasn't suitable for little ears.

"Uncle Jake," Emma said, tugging on his shirt sleeve.

"Yeah?" He shifted to give her his full attention.

"Maybe you should do something nice for Fred, so she doesn't get angry at the dough anymore."

Jake forced back a grin. He'd spent enough time

around Emma to know the tone she used meant she was serious.

Braden coughed and pounded on his chest after nearly choking on his bite of chicken. "Did she say dough?" he asked Casey.

"I'm afraid so," Casey said with a nod.

Jake had no idea what Emma was talking about but had a bad feeling that it had something to do with him. He gave Casey a questioning glance.

"I'll fill you both in later," she said.

"Something nice, huh?" Jake asked Emma. "That's actually a good idea." He tweaked her nose, eliciting a grin. Maybe the little one was right. Maybe if he did something for Fred, something that only she would appreciate, he might stand a chance of having the conversation they so desperately needed to have and win her over in the process.

"I don't suppose you'd know what I could give her, do you?" Jake asked. Emma was more perceptive than most children her age, and maybe she'd gleaned something that might be useful.

She tapped her chin and wrinkled her brow the way some adults do when they're concentrating. It was the cutest thing, and Jake fought hard not to chuckle. Finally, Emma said, "I do", then leaned closer as if she wanted to share a secret. "I heard her tell Grainger that she wished she had a barn for her plants."

It seemed sharing thoughts with the animals on the property was gaining popularity. It sounded like an odd request. Jake raised a brow and asked, "A barn? Are you sure?"

"Uh-huh." Emma bobbed her head. "She said she needed a place to keep her plants so they would stay safe and grow better. You know, like how we have a place for Lexi's animals."

"I'll bet Fred meant a greenhouse," Casey said. "She's mentioned it a couple of times."

"That's a great idea, Ems," Jake said, then tickled her until she squealed.

The more Jake thought about it, the more he agreed with Emma. Finding a layout online and acquiring supplies wouldn't be difficult. The hard part was finding a place to hide the greenhouse from Fred until it was completed.

Maybe things weren't as bleak as he believed. At least that's what Jake thought until Fred entered the room from the hallway leading to the kitchen carrying a covered metal pan with a tall male toting a large basket of biscuits and following close behind her. The distance between them was way too close for Jake's liking or his bear's.

With most of the guests being shifters with high metabolisms, the food on the buffet table went quickly. Fred did a great job monitoring consumption and replacing containers when needed.

Jake's problem wasn't with the pan Fred was carrying. It was the tall male following her that bothered him. He could dismiss the fact that the male was helping Fred bring out food, but the way he stared at her backside was hard to ignore. He gripped the edge of the table, urging his animal to stop growling.

"Uncle Jake," Emma said, patting his thigh and giving him the distraction he needed to prevent the oncoming shift. "I don't like the guy that is helping Fred."

At the moment, neither did Jake. Despite the sharp, angled nose and arrogant stride, the male's muscular build and other facial features would attract most females. Even from this distance, Jake detected the prowess of a shifter, and if he had to make a guess without catching his scent first, he'd say the male's animal was a wolf.

Fred excelled at masking her emotions, but Jake had spent enough time observing her from a distance to know that the subtle straightening of her spine reflected her discomfort with the male's presence. Her reaction brought out his protective nature and made handling his bear even more difficult.

Jake blamed himself for the current situation. If he'd acknowledged Fred as his mate sooner and proclaimed his intentions, he'd be the one helping her instead of watching from a distance and fighting with his bear.

"Emma, honey, he's a guest," Casey said, her voice kind, yet stern. "It's not all right to talk badly about other people. Do you understand?"

"Yeah." Emma stubbornly folded her arms across her chest. "But I still don't like him."

Braden glanced over his shoulder and frowned. "Isn't he the guy who showed up without a reservation?"

"Yes, but still…" Casey gave Emma another motherly look.

Emma was sweet-natured, and it was rare for her to show defiance. Jake might agree with the child, but Casey was right. He didn't know much about parenting, but they all did their best to teach Emma to be polite and kind to others. Jake suspected that something must have happened to cause her to have a strong reaction to the male.

"Emma," Jake said, giving her arm a soothing rub. "Did he do something to you?" If the male had said or done anything, even slightly inappropriate, Jake was going to lose the last remnants of patience he possessed and bring out his claws.

"No, but what if Fred likes him?" she asked with a sniff. "Then she might leave us."

Jake wanted to know where Emma had gotten the notion about Fred leaving, but with her eyes glistening with moisture, he was afraid asking the wrong questions might cause her to burst into tears. "Ems, I promise I'm not going to let that happen."

"Okay." Emma was too short to reach his neck, so her hug barely covered the sides of his waist. "Thanks, Uncle Jake. You're the best."

Jake pressed a gentle kiss to Emma's forehead as he got to his feet. "Maybe I'll go over there and see if Fred needs some help." He shrugged off the look that passed between

Braden and Casey as he got to his feet.

"This isn't going to be good, is it?" Jake overheard Casey ask Braden after he left. "Do you think we should…" Jake didn't like being responsible for the concern he'd heard in Casey's voice, but it wasn't going to keep him away from Fred or prevent the male from bothering her.

"He needs to do this," Jake heard Braden say and envisioned him placing a comforting hand on his mate's arm.

Jake was pretty sure his cousin would let him handle things as long as he controlled his bear. Casey was one of the most determined females Jake had ever met. Even Braden wouldn't be able to stop her if she decided that Jake needed her help.

CHAPTER SEVEN

Fred was quite capable of doing her job and had no idea why Conrad thought she needed help restocking the dinner buffet. He was a guest and had no business being in the lodge's kitchen. The first time could've been an understandable mistake, but not the second.

The sign for employees only was still posted on the wall and easily visible, so she didn't understand why he didn't remain in the dining hall with everyone else. Besides her bedroom in the house behind the lodge, the kitchen was her private domicile, and she resented his intrusion.

Conrad seemed like an okay enough guy, though maybe a little too nice. It was as if he was trying too hard to make a good impression. Gaining a male's interest would've been flattering, but from the moment he'd arrived at the ranch without an invitation, wariness had prickled Fred's skin, and her fox had paced uneasily every time she saw him.

"You really don't need to help," Fred said, fighting the temptation to rip the basket containing biscuits from the arm where he clutched it against his chest. His guest status, muscular build, and the added strength of his wolf were strong deterrents.

"I don't mind," Conrad said, smiling. "Helping beautiful females is the gentlemanly thing to do."

Well, Fred minded. She also wished she could figure out what the male was up to because she had a hard time believing he was motivated by manners.

She'd been tempted to tell him she wasn't available with hopes that he'd leave her alone. But knowing Jake was her mate didn't mean she was actually mated. That wouldn't happen unless the infuriating male got around to actually acknowledging their connection and marking her with a bite that signified a lasting bond and let everyone in the shifter world know she was taken.

After Celia's arrival, Jake's actions grew more confusing than normal. Males didn't usually offer to help their mothers unpack. Fred sensed it had been an excuse, that he hadn't expected to find Celia in the kitchen. Had her intuition been right? Had he been looking for her? Excitement rose in her chest. It had taken some time, but the interaction she had with Jake in the garden assured her that she'd never be satisfied with anyone else.

Pushing Jake from her thoughts, she focused her attention on Conrad. Other than being noticeably rude, she'd done everything she could think of to get him to leave. Since that hadn't worked, maybe now would be a good time to find out his real reason for coming to the ranch. "Earlier, you mentioned being in the area. Were you traveling anywhere specific?" Not to appear too nosy, Fred gave him her back as she slipped on some mitts and removed a metal container from the oven where she'd been keeping it warm.

As she lifted the lid to check on the contents, the aroma of baked beans filled the air. This dish, along with her crispy chicken, was popular with the guests, so she always prepared extra pans of both on the days she served them.

"Not really," Conrad said. "I thought I might head out to California when I leave here. Maybe check out the beaches."

Fred had grown up in the coastal state and tried not to show a reaction. She didn't want to dismiss his choice of destination as a coincidence until she'd gleaned additional information. "Sounds like fun."

"How about you?" he asked. "Have you lived here all your life, or did you grow up somewhere else?"

Conrad's questions might sound innocent, but Fred got the impression he was purposely searching for information, and there was no way she was going to give him any. "Why do you ask?" She tightened her grip on the pan and headed for the hallway.

"Mostly out of curiosity," he said, following after her. "I travel quite a bit with my job and find it interesting how people end up in different places."

"Oh, yeah. What kind of work do you do?" He possessed the charm of a salesperson but didn't seem the type. If Fred had to guess his profession, she'd say bounty hunter or private investigator.

"A variety of things."

His vague answer was a disappointment, yet not unexpected. If he had an agenda for visiting the ranch, Fred doubted he'd be willing to share it with her.

Conrad spent the entire trip down the corridor crowding her personal space and making her increasingly uncomfortable. Fred did her best to keep at least two feet between them, too afraid her fox would start growling if they accidentally touched. Adding to her annoyance was his heated gaze, something she could feel without glancing over her shoulder. If he didn't quit staring at her backside, he was going to be wearing the basket of biscuits instead of carrying them.

When they reached the end of the buffet tables, she set the covered metal pan she held sideways on top of several others, then removed her mitts.

"Where would you like me to put this?" Conrad asked.

She dismissed her sarcastic response, but Jake appeared

before she could use a polite one.

"Here, let me take that for you," Jake said, snatching the basket out of Conrad's hands and stepping between him and Fred. Unless she was distracted, her fox could always sense when he was near. She hadn't needed her animal's help because she'd already scanned the dining hall and spotted him sitting with Braden and Casey at a table on the other side of the room.

"Jake, what—,"

"Sorry, Fred," he said, cutting her off before she could ask him what the heck he was doing. "I couldn't get here any sooner to help." His gaze never leaving Conrad as he spoke.

Fred had no idea what he was talking about. Jake was a ranch employee, but his duties had never extended to assisting her in the past. She couldn't deny that a part of her was happy to see him, but another part was annoyed by his interference.

If it had been any other time and any other male who'd treated her as if she couldn't handle herself, Fred would have been furious and kicked them in the shin or shown them her claws. But it was Jake, and when his deep voice rippled across her skin, it had a calming effect. Even more so for her fox, who was making happy noises and wanted to drape herself across his shoulders.

Her irritating animal might be appeased, but Fred certainly wasn't. If they hadn't been under the scrutiny of guests and Jake's mother, she would've told him exactly how she felt about his overprotective behavior.

"Fred, who is this guy?" Conrad, disappointed by the interruption, growled loud enough to be overheard. He sidestepped to peer at her around Jake.

"Conrad, this is Jake." Fred had to answer from behind Jake's back because he'd mirrored Conrad's move, so he couldn't get anywhere near her.

"Sorry, I should've introduced myself," Jake said, tucking the basket in the cradle of his left arm, then sticking out his hand. "I'm a member of the family and also the staff."

It was a good thing he hadn't said anything about being Fred's mate; otherwise, he definitely would've gotten kicked. Jake sounded pleasant enough, but when he refused to lower his arm, she didn't think his gesture was meant to be friendly.

Fred couldn't see Jake's face, but she didn't miss the glare Conrad leveled at him.

After a moment of scrutiny, he accepted Jake's challenge. Their shared grip lasted longer than normal, and Fred believed she'd witnessed an unspoken display of dominance. If the males had been outside without any observers, their animals would've most likely gotten involved.

"Hey, Mr. Morgan," Casey said, holding Emma's hand as she casually strolled up to the other side of the table. She acted as if she hadn't noticed the confrontation or Conrad's attempt to pull away from Jake so both males could face her. "How are you enjoying your stay?"

"Fine, thanks," Conrad said, his answer a little too brusque, which he immediately corrected by adding, "Please, call me Conrad."

Fred would've believed Casey's arrival hadn't been intentional if Emma wasn't smiling at Jake like he'd just completed a heroic deed. The wink Jake gave the child earned him an even wider grin, and Fred wondered if something had transpired between the two of them. Something that had to do with her.

Casey took the responsibility of running the ranch seriously. Not all the guests were shifters, so everyone's welfare was at the top of her list. It usually meant stopping things before they headed in a bad direction.

She had to know, or at least suspect, what was going on between Jake and Conrad, which would explain her proactive intervention. When Braden walked past them a few minutes later, carrying a stack of empty plates, which he placed in a bin designated for dirty dishes, Fred knew it wasn't an accident.

Casey must have told Braden about Conrad and the concerns they'd discussed earlier. Fred hoped her friend had kept her word about not saying anything to Jake. If Casey had, then Jake's motivation to help her was his own, which made her stomach flutter.

Fred also noticed Jake's mother and aunt sitting a few tables away with several guests. They seemed to be enjoying their conversation, but Fred caught Celia glancing in their direction.

If Celia suspected that Fred was Jake's match, the topic never came up during their earlier visit. Did her satisfied smirk mean she was proud of her son's action, and more importantly, that she approved of Fred being his mate? Fred's thoughts drifted to her parents. If they were still alive, would they also approve of the match?

"This is my husband, Braden." Casey's introduction to Conrad pulled Fred from her musings. "And I believe you've already met Emma." She smiled down at the child and gave her small hand a squeeze.

"Nice to meet you," Braden said, foregoing an introductory handshake.

"Are you two related?" Conrad asked, pointing at Jake, then Braden.

"Cousins," Jake said, grinning.

Shifters could recognize each other's animals. Conrad must have sensed that Jake and Braden were bears. The family resemblance was quite noticeable when the two males stood next to each other, so guessing they were related was an easy assumption to make. Other than stuffing his hands in his pockets, which could've been to hide the unwanted appearance of claws, the wolf didn't show any signs of feeling outnumbered.

"If you haven't tried the food yet, you won't be disappointed," Braden patted his stomach. "I was thinking about grabbing some more chicken myself. Care to try some?" He pulled two clean plates off a nearby stack and offered one to Conrad. Braden had asked politely, but his tone held a note of insistence.

"Sure, why not?" Conrad took the plate and stepped around Braden, Casey, and Emma until he was standing across the table from Fred. "Seeing how you went to a lot of trouble and all." He ignored Jake's growl and grinned at Fred. "Maybe we can talk again later…when you're not working."

"We'll have to see," Fred said. She didn't want to spend any time with Conrad but feared that telling him no in front of Jake would only encourage him to pursue her more.

After filling their plates, Braden strolled away with Casey and Emma while Conrad found a table on the opposite side of the room.

Once Fred was alone with Jake, he asked, "What do you mean, you'll have to see?"

"I don't think that's any of your business," Fred said as she replaced the empty container, then moved along the back of the tables, lifting lids and forcing herself to remember which items needed to be refilled. Usually, it was a simple task, but concentrating was difficult with Jake standing so close and watching her movements.

"What do you mean it's none of my concern?" Jake kept his voice low, but Fred still detected his underlying irritation.

Any reply Fred made would most likely lead to discussing their mate status and inevitably an argument. She was torn between answering his question and ignoring him completely. Luckily, she was spared from doing either when a male voice asked, "Young man, I don't suppose you'd be willing to share those biscuits, would you?"

Fred looked up from what she was doing to find Hudson Attwater. He was an elderly coyote shifter who'd recently arrived and was celebrating his second honeymoon with his mate Mallory.

Jake glanced at the basket as if he'd forgotten he was still holding it. "Sure," he said, then walked over and placed it on a nearby table. When Jake returned, Fred grabbed the empty tin and shoved it at him. "You said you wanted to help, so here. You can take this back to the kitchen." She snatched up the mitts and hurried for the hallway.

Fred silently cursed Jake's nerve, her annoyance mounting all the way to the kitchen. It would've been nice if she'd had some dough handy to take out her frustration. She had no idea if Jake would follow her, so after tossing the mitts on the counter, she stepped over to the sink, intent on giving the dirty dishes an excessive washing.

As she leaned over to grab the bottle of liquid dish soap from the lower cabinet, heat spread throughout her body. When she stood back up, Jake had placed the pan on the center island and was standing right behind her, his dark eyes filled with concern…and longing.

"Fred," he said, running a hand through his hair as he took a step toward her. "We need to talk."

She didn't think telling him it was about time would be constructive, so instead, she said, "You're right, we do." She hadn't gotten a chance to release her frustration yet, so she placed the bottle on the counter to keep from chucking it at his head. "I'd like to go first."

"Okay," he said, his tone wary.

"I'm not sure what you were trying to prove out there, but in case you weren't aware, I *can* take care of myself." Fred poked Jake in the chest. "You don't get to strut around like some white knight and treat me as if I were a damsel in distress." Fred had blurted out the first thing she could think of, which was based on Jake's horsemanship skills and how good he looked in a saddle. Once the words were out, she realized how ironic they sounded.

Apparently, judging by Jake's amused grin, he did as well. "You know, you're awfully cute when you're mad."

"Don't change the subject," Fred huffed, taking a step

backward.

"I'm serious," Jake said, easing a little closer. "I think you're absolutely gorgeous." He pushed a loose strand behind her ear, a tingle starting where his fingertips brushed against her skin. "I also happen to think you're right."

Jake was taller than her, so Fred had to tip her head back to see his face. "You do?" she asked, astonished by his response.

"Yes." He placed his hands on her hips, the warmth from his palms radiating through the fabric of her shirt. "I may have overreacted a bit."

"You think," Fred said, not quite ready to forgive him yet.

"It's what males do when they care about their mates."

"Mates?" Even if she'd wanted to ask more questions, Jake's mouth capturing hers prevented it.

The kiss was gentle yet possessive at the same time. Fred moaned, skimmed her palms across his broad shoulders, and leaned into him as if she'd been starving for his touch her whole life.

When he finally released her, he tipped her chin and held her gaze. "Yes."

"Whoa, sorry," Kelsey said, appearing in the entryway carrying a bin of dirty dishes. "Am I interrupting?"

Fred had no idea how long her friend had been standing in the doorway or if she'd witnessed the kiss. She was embarrassed at being caught, but escape was impossible with Jake still holding her hips.

"Nope," Jake said, never taking his eyes off Fred. He pressed his cheek against hers and whispered, "You can get mad at me and avoid me all you want, but I'm not going anywhere." He pulled away from Fred, and after giving Kelsey a nod, which included a grin, he disappeared from the room.

Fred's heart raced and wouldn't stop, no matter how much air she gulped. She wasn't sure what shocked her the most. The fact that Jake's kiss left her gasping and wanting more or that he'd officially proclaimed them mates.

CHAPTER EIGHT

Fred paced the floor in front of the kitchen counter in the house she shared with the sisters and contemplated the recent changes in her life. It was still early, so she had some time before heading over to the lodge and preparing breakfast for the guests. While she waited for the coffee to finish brewing, memories of the time she'd spent with Jake played through her mind.

Until last night, her emotions fluctuated from being exhilarated at finding her mate to being disappointed that he didn't want her. She hadn't gotten a restful night of sleep since he'd first arrived at the ranch. After his private announcement, Fred finally had an answer, and it had taken her the longest time to unwind enough to close her eyes. Once she did, she'd fallen into a deep slumber filled with fantasies about Jake in her bed and being wrapped in his arms.

If she hadn't been deep in thought, she would've heard Casey's approach and wouldn't have jumped when her friend said her name. Even her fox, who'd been snarling at Fred for days to claim her mate, had finally settled into a semi-content state and hadn't noticed Casey either.

"Uh, morning," Fred said. The coffee was ready, so she

grabbed two mugs out of the cupboard and filled one for each of them.

"Is everything okay?" Casey asked as she took the cup Fred offered her. "I was a little worried after what happened with Conrad and Jake."

"Fine," Fred said, running her fingertip along her lower lip, remembering the kiss she'd shared with Jake. She wanted to believe he'd done it because he cared, but his past actions kept popping up, and she couldn't shake the feeling that he'd intervened to protect her. Nothing more.

"I'm curious," Fred said. "Did you tell Jake about our suspicions regarding Conrad?"

"No, I never said a word," Casey said, then blew on her coffee. "Why?"

The tension straining the muscles in Fred's shoulders slackened. Before she could answer, Lexi burst into the room with her usual boisterousness. She looked at Fred and practically shrieked. "Oh my gosh. Jake kissed you, didn't he?"

Fred's skin heated, and she didn't need a mirror to know her cheeks were as dark as her freckles.

Lexi eased around Casey, then filled a mug for herself. "I was afraid after Jake got in Conrad's face last night that claws would be flying between the two of you. I know they would've if it was a male I liked. Or at least words anyway since I can't shift. But still, judging by your complexion, I'd say you guys finally talked about your relationship."

Another wave of warmth surged across Fred's skin. Words had been shared all right but weren't nearly as memorable as their body actions. Something she wasn't about to mention to either female.

"Lexi," Casey said, raising her voice several levels above normal to get her sister's attention.

Fred knew Lexi meant well, but sometimes it would be nice if she controlled her tendency to share her observations with others. Specifically when they concerned Fred.

"Morning," Kelsey said, yawning as she sauntered into the room, followed by Violet and Celia. She took in everyone's expressions and asked, "What did we miss?"

Fred was glad that Kelsey was reserved about personal topics and that she hadn't said anything about interrupting Jake and her.

"Fred was about to tell us how she and Jake are together now." Lexi leaned against the counter next to Casey and grinned before blowing on her coffee.

"We aren't together," Fred said with some uncertainty. Jake might have told her they were mates, even kissed her senseless, but that didn't necessarily mean he planned to follow through on exploring a relationship with the prospects of claiming her.

"Oh, honey," Celia said, moving further into the room. "That boy of mine is crazy about you." She walked over and cupped Fred's cheeks. "Of course, you're together."

Fred groaned. "Well, up until last night, he had a funny way of showing he was even interested." She'd been reluctant to discuss Jake with his mother and couldn't believe she'd blurted out her annoyance with the female's son.

She liked Celia, and if things worked out with Jake, they'd be family. Since her parents' death, Fred missed having an older female she could talk to about these kinds of things. Celia and Violet seemed close, and Fred wondered if she'd gain a confidant with Braden's mother as well.

"Jake's father was the same way. He can be quite the charmer, but it took him forever to get around to telling me I was his mate." Celia grinned as if recalling some special memories.

"Did you say anything to him?" Fred asked, realizing the similarities in their situations and wanting to know if Celia had handled things differently. Fred didn't think Jake's mother had been on the run from a relative at the time, which for Fred, had played an influential role in her decision-making when it came to her mate.

"Of course not. I figured if the silly male wanted me in his life, then it was up to him to do most of the work. The connection between us was strong from the start. I knew he was the one from the moment our eyes met. And the first time we touched,"—Celia fanned herself—"my body tingled for hours."

"Really?" Lexi asked. "Care to share with those of us who haven't found our mate yet?"

"Celia, that won't be necessary," Kelsey snapped and glared at Lexi. "Some of us would prefer not to hear private details."

For Kelsey's sake, Fred wanted to change the subject. Her friend had taken being rejected by her ex hard, and it couldn't be easy to see or hear about others' success stories. She might put on a brave front for everyone around her, but Fred knew it would be a long time before Kelsey let anyone near her heart again. If ever.

Celia wasn't ready to end the discussion and flashed Fred a knowing grin. "I imagine you're going through pretty much the same thing with my son, aren't you?"

All Fred could do was nod. It was as if the older female could see through to her soul, tap into her emotions, and extract her thoughts.

"Give him time," Celia said. "It will be well worth the wait."

"How so?" Lexi asked.

"With any luck, Jake will take after his father. Let's just say my mate knows how to be romantic in and out of the bedroom." Celia blew out a breath and wiggled her eyebrows. "If you know what I mean."

Braden ambled into the room, caught the last of what Celia had said, and stopped. Before Casey and Braden got married, only females occupied the house. Before then, Fred didn't think much of walking around outside work hours in a nightshirt and socks.

Out of respect for her friend, and because she didn't

want Braden to catch her in a state of undress, she made sure to put on a T-shirt and sweat pants before leaving her room. Shoes were optional since she occasionally got up early to let her fox run. On those days, she waited until she was in the woods and a reasonable distance from the house before shedding her clothes to transform.

Braden glanced around uncomfortably as if weighing his options. "This is not a discussion I want to be a part of," he mumbled as he slowly backed out of the kitchen. "I'll get some coffee over at the lodge."

Lexi shot a sidelong look at Casey, then giggled. "I think Celia has officially traumatized your mate."

"He'll be fine," Violet said. "Braden's father and I have shocked him plenty over the years, and he still turned out fine."

"No disagreements on the way he turned out, but I wouldn't mind hearing more about the events that molded him," Casey said.

"I look forward to the conversation." Violet gave Casey a conspiratorial wink. "Though I'm not sure how happy Braden will be once he finds out."

"Then it will have to be our little secret," Casey said.

"I should go start my prep," Fred said, then drained the last of her coffee and set the cup in the sink.

"Casey, do you suppose you can spare Fred after breakfast this morning?" Celia asked in a tone that sounded a little too sweet and less innocent.

"Why?" Casey asked, raising a brow. Fred was glad to see that she wasn't the only one suspicious of the request.

"We wanted to do some shopping," Celia said, glancing at Violet, who was smiling and bobbing her head. "I want to make Jake and Braden's favorite dish and was hoping Fred could help me find the additional ingredients I need."

It hadn't taken Celia long to figure out that anything to do with food preparation was Fred's biggest weakness. Actually, she had two. The first was cooking, and the second, which was slowly taking the lead after recent events, was Jake. She wouldn't admit it to anyone, least of all Jake, but she'd been keeping a close watch on his selections at the buffet table and taking notes.

Learning his favorite foods, especially from Celia, who'd had plenty of practice preparing them for him, had a lot of appeal. Fred might be excited by the prospect but wasn't willing to dismiss her duties and asked, "What about lunch?"

"Go and have a good time," Casey said, tipping her head in the direction of her sisters. "I'm sure the three of us can handle things while you're gone."

CHAPTER NINE

Jake didn't care who was making the loud rapping noise or calling his name. They'd interrupted the dream he was having about kissing Fred, among other things, and would suffer some claw action, or at the very least, a well-placed smack to the side of their head.

As far as he was concerned, having a pillow career off his face was enough to end someone's life. With a snarl, Jake forced his eyes open and spotted Braden standing in the doorway, searching for something else he could throw. Not that Jake blamed him. His cousin had learned the hard way not to stand too close if he was going to wake him up before he was ready to get out of bed.

"Are you planning on getting up some time today?" Braden asked, leaning against the frame.

If Braden was there pestering him, then there was a good chance Jake had overslept. A glance at his alarm clock confirmed that he had twenty minutes before he was supposed to head out on the trail ride with Kelsey and some of the guests.

"Maybe," Jake growled, then whipped back the comforter and pushed out of bed. There wasn't enough time for a shower, so getting dressed, combing his mussed hair, and brushing his teeth would have to suffice. It also meant skipping breakfast and missing out on seeing Fred, which added to his already surly mood. He grabbed a shirt and a pair of pants from the closet and headed for the bathroom.

Most of Jake's exhaustion stemmed from staying up past midnight. He'd spent his time searching for the perfect greenhouse design. In the end, he'd compiled several different layouts into one that he thought Fred would like. He'd also found some spare lumber and planned to check with Casey to make sure she didn't have a problem with him using it. Whatever he couldn't find lying around, he'd order later today.

Before that, he'd covertly tracked Conrad, which was uneventful since the male retired to his cabin shortly after leaving the dining hall. Jake could understand the wolf's interest in Fred if he'd been a regular guest and had interacted with her in a normal manner. He didn't believe in coincidences, and several things about the male didn't make sense. The first was showing up at a secluded ranch without a reservation.

None of the sisters could shift, but they all had shifter blood and could sense things that most humans couldn't. After Kelsey caught the aftermath of Jake kissing Fred, she'd tracked him down and told him how Conrad had made her uneasy from the moment he'd entered the lodge. So much so that she'd made sure to tell Jake about Conrad's immediate interest in Fred when he'd first arrived.

Not only was the male paying extra attention to Jake's mate, but he'd ignored the sign preventing guest access to the kitchen to do it. The information he received from Kelsey increased his wariness and prompted the additional surveillance.

Even if Jake hadn't noticed Fred's discomfort around Conrad, he still would've sought him out. There more discreet ways of handling competition. Pulling the male aside and explaining that Fred was his mate would've been the simplest. Yet logic had escaped him, and he'd reacted like any other bear who wanted to protect their female.

Jake knew he couldn't say anything to Conrad in front of Fred, not without upsetting her, so he'd gone with the less noticeable show of dominance via a handshake. An action that didn't seem to make any difference to the wolf. Jake didn't think Conrad's interest had anything to do with Fred being an attractive female. Until he could figure out the other male's intentions, he planned to continue monitoring his actions.

His bear had a differing opinion. He thought they should get Conrad alone and show him what happened to anyone who dared to sniff around their mate. The animal was convinced that a few well-placed swipes would have him leaving in no time. If Conrad wasn't a paying guest, Jake might have agreed with him. He didn't want to do anything that might jeopardize the ranch's reputation, not without being able to justify it first.

With Fred already on his mind, Jake's thoughts drifted to their interaction the night before. He'd known when he went to the kitchen that he'd made a mistake when he'd confronted Conrad and had planned to apologize. He hadn't realized how badly the situation had gotten until Fred ranted about being able to take care of herself.

The short speech he'd rehearsed in the hallway evaporated the moment he stepped into the room. Kissing her, something he'd wanted to do for days, was the only thing he could think of that would let Fred know she was his mate and to make sure she had no doubts about his intentions. Of course, his bear had no interest in dealing with human propriety and wanted Jake to claim her the instant their lips touched.

When Braden didn't leave right away, an uneasy feeling crept into Jake's chest. He left the door partially open and asked, "Is there a reason you're still hanging around?" He knew he wouldn't like the answer before he asked the question.

"I thought you might want to know our mothers had Fred take them into town to go shopping," Braden said.

Having Jake's mate spend time alone with two meddling females meant trouble in a monumental way. When he'd left Fred alone with Celia the day before, he thought he'd gotten off easy, but if his mother and her sister had taken Fred on a road trip, they were up to something. Something possibly worse than grilling Fred about her thoughts on children.

"What?" He had one pant leg partially pulled up but stopped to peer around the door and glare at his cousin. "How could you let that happen?"

"Like I had a choice," Braden grumbled. "*Your* mate's an independent female and quite capable of making her own decisions. Besides, Casey thought it was a great idea. And as much as I'd like to give you my support, there's no way I'm going to get on my mate's bad side."

The satisfaction Jake felt after hearing his cousin refer to Fred as his mate was fleeting. He couldn't blame Braden for not wanting to get involved. Besides being a darned good cook, Fred also had a temper. Bears liked their food and knew better than to upset the person preparing the dishes.

If things were reversed, Jake would think twice before crossing the fiery little fox. Not that any amount of understanding was going to help his current predicament.

After muttering several curse words, he slammed the door and finished dressing. Normally, he looked forward to assisting Kelsey with the trail rides, but worrying about Fred being away from him for so long diminished the possibility of future enjoyment.

His concern wasn't solely based on Fred's personal welfare. Being bears, his mother and aunt would look after her as if she was their own cub. He was worried that a few hours spent with the females might undo the headway he'd made with her the night before.

CHAPTER TEN

After the extremely embarrassing conversation with Jake's mother and aunt in the kitchen, Fred hurried through her usual routine of picking vegetables from the garden, then preparing breakfast for the guests. She was disappointed that Jake hadn't made an appearance at either location. Things between them were tenuous, and it was hard not to experience self-doubt and worry that his proclamation was an attempt to keep her from staying mad at him.

Her fox reacted differently to the situation. She was convinced that Jake had overslept and thought they should wake him up. Maybe crawl into bed with him.

Conrad had shown up with smiles and flirtatious quips as if his confrontation with Jake had never happened. It was a good thing he'd decided to stay on the guest's side of the buffet table and out of her kitchen; otherwise, he might not have left unscathed.

By the time she had Celia and Violet loaded into the truck and was driving on the road leading to town, Fred's frustration hadn't subsided. If Violet and Celia were aware of her irritated state, they'd pretended not to notice. They'd chatted pretty much non-stop during the entire trip, a majority of the topics centered around Jake, which Fred assumed were for her benefit.

The drive passed quickly, and shortly after spotting the city limit sign, Fred noticed Celia scanning the buildings lining Waynesrock's main street as if she was searching for something specific. Though Violet had yet to point out any places she'd like to visit, Fred had no doubt she'd been doing the same thing from the truck's back seat.

"Do you mind if we stop by the mercantile first," Fred asked. "Lexi wanted me to pick up some pellets for Darla." Lexi had recently acquired several other goats but hadn't named them yet.

"Not at all," Violet said. "But who's Darla?"

"She's the goat, right?" Celia asked Fred. "The one Emma said likes to chew on clothes."

"Yes," Fred giggled. "The puppies are in the same barn, and I'm sure Emma will want you to see them as well. So dress accordingly."

"In other words, wear something that could end up in the trash," Violet said.

"Pretty much," Fred said as she slowed the truck to pull into the mercantile's lot. She loved shopping at the country-style store. She hadn't been there in a while because cooking and taking care of the garden took up most of her time. After stepping through the doorway, seeing the bins filled with fresh produce, and getting a whiff of various baked goods, she was glad Celia and Violet had suggested she go with them.

The place had a welcoming, homey feel. Most of the shelves filling the center of the room were made of wood. Two of the walls were papered with a tan and dark brown design, the hardwood floors adding to the ambiance.

The rectangular building housing the store served dual purposes. A long wall with a single entryway divided the interior. One side was a grocery store, and the other was dedicated to livestock supplies. The shelves that ran through the center of the room were lined with smaller items like water buckets and feeders. Several pallets had been placed on the floor toward the back and contained medium to large bags of food for smaller animals such as goats and chickens.

"This place is amazing," Celia said, her smile widening the more she perused the stocked shelves. "It looks like they should have everything I need."

Fred already had the spices Celia would need on hand at the ranch, but not the meat and additional vegetables.

"If you can't find something, don't be afraid to ask," a tall, middle-aged man said as he moved around the corner of a long row of shelves. Thinning strands covered a partially bald head. The brown and white checkered shirt, jeans, and boots that showed signs of wear, made him fit right in with the store's environment. "Good morning, Fred," he said, flashing her a wide smile.

"Hey, Roy," Fred replied.

"Who are your friends?" he asked.

"This is Braden's mother, Violet." Fred raised a hand as she spoke. "And Celia, Jake's mom." Braden and Jake had been to the mercantile a few times since making a home at the ranch, so no additional explanation was required. Like many people who'd settled in the area, Roy was a shifter, specifically a wolf.

"Glad to meet you, ladies," he said. "Nice pair of boys you got there. I was happy to hear Casey finally found her mate. Now we need to find someone for Fred."

Having raised two daughters of his own, Roy didn't have a problem extending his fatherly advice to Fred and her friends. She was fond of the older male but would rather not discuss her personal life with him in public or anywhere else for that matter.

"We most certainly do," Celia said, draping an arm across Fred's shoulder.

Fred was shocked and relieved that Jake's mother hadn't embarrassed her by announcing her connection with her son. An act that had earned Celia her admiration and respect. Even though Fred hadn't known the females long, she had to admit she did enjoy spending time with them.

"Now, about those supplies," Celia said, then headed toward the cooling units containing meat.

"While you two do that, I'm going to get some pellets for Lexi's goats and load them in the truck," Fred said.

"We shouldn't be too long and will meet you outside when we're done," Violet said, then took off after Celia.

Fred supported Lexi's endeavor to adopt unwanted animals and always liked to see if there was anything new her friend might need to help with their care. The bag of pellets wasn't very heavy, so after she'd done some shopping of her own, Fred loaded it in the bed of the truck.

She'd parked the vehicle with the front end butting up against a pedestrian sidewalk, which gave her an unobstructed view of the town's main street. As she snapped the tailgate into place, she glimpsed Conrad's jeep. He was going slower than the posted speed limit as if he was searching for something specific.

Fred didn't think his arrival was an accident. Conrad hadn't mentioned knowing anyone in the area. Was it possible he was here to meet someone? Maybe someone like Harlan.

She hadn't seen Harlan or any of the males who worked for him, but she hadn't been looking for them either. As curious as Fred was to find out why Conrad was in town, a part of her, the side governed by her fox's instincts, was screaming at her to avoid being seen by him.

Her animal rarely gave her bad advice, so she ducked behind the back of the vehicle, peering over the frame to make sure he kept on driving. If Conrad was searching for the ranch's truck or the easily recognizable logo painted on the front doors, the vehicles parked on either side were blocking his view.

Unfortunately, her attempt to hide hadn't gone

unnoticed. Celia and Violet picked that moment to leave the store, each carrying several plastic bags hooked on their wrists. "Fred, what are you doing?" Celia asked, concern in her voice. "Is everything all right?"

Fred ignored her racing heart and pretended that she hadn't squeaked from being startled. Other than her intuition, she had no proof that Conrad was up to something sinister. She didn't want to worry Celia and Violet unnecessarily by telling them about him. "Everything's fine," Fred said, then gave the tailgate a pat as if double-checking to make sure it was secure. "Let me help you with those." She hurried to unlock and open the doors.

It didn't take long for everyone to get inside and be on their way. Before Fred could pull out onto the main street, Violet asked, "Would you mind driving through town before we head back?"

"Sure," Fred said, turning in the opposite direction and hoping that wherever Celia and Violet wanted to go wouldn't have them running into Conrad.

"Fred, do you remember me telling you about Jake's father and how it took him the longest time to get around to telling me I was his mate?" Celia asked.

"Yeah," Fred said, stretching out the word. She refrained from mentioning that they'd only discussed the topic a few hours ago. Fred had no idea what had prompted Celia to revisit the subject but sensed there was more to the story. "Why?" she asked, trying to appease the uneasy feeling that Celia's reason had to do with Jake and her.

"It might have taken him a lot longer if I hadn't given him the occasional nudge," Celia said, a hint of exasperation in her voice.

"Really?" Fred didn't hold back her astonishment.

"Of course."

Fred shouldn't have been surprised to hear that the older female resorted to manipulation to get her way, not after witnessing the persuasive techniques she'd used to get her to accompany them into town.

"Jake has been searching for his mate ever since he graduated high school. It's all he ever talked about." Celia tapped her chin. "If I had to guess, I'd say now that he's found you, he's afraid he'll mess it up. So in his mind, not doing anything is the best course of action."

"Which we all know has been failing epically," Violet said.

"At least until last night," Fred said, willing to give Jake points for finally talking to her about being mates and a gold star for the breath-stealing kiss.

"Yes, but I think we need to move things along a bit, don't you?" Fred realized Celia was asking Violet and not her.

"I agree," Violet said. "I assume you have something in mind."

"Actually, I do," Celia said, glancing out the window, then patting the dashboard. "Violet, how do you feel about stopping at that dress shop up ahead?" She pointed at the Barbary Fashion Boutique located on the next block.

"Considering there's a dance at the ranch tomorrow night, I think that's a wonderful idea," Violet said. "I'm not sure we have anything suitable to wear."

The females appeared to be prepared for any occasion. Fred found it hard to believe they hadn't packed anything appropriate for a low-key dance.

Celia shifted in her seat so she could speak directly to Violet. "Maybe we can find something nice for Fred to wear as well."

Fred tightened her grip on the steering wheel and thought about all the ways she could throttle Casey when they got back. Now she understood why her friend hadn't balked when Celia asked if she could spare Fred for a few hours. She'd been their co-conspirator.

The sisters had been trying for months to get Fred to attend the weekly Friday night dance the ranch hosted.

And every week, Fred turned them down. Sitting near the entrance and helping collect tickets from the townsfolk who attended was the closest she'd ever gotten to the dance floor.

It wasn't that Fred didn't like to dance or even that she didn't know how. It was having to wear something nice, like a dress or skirt, that she had a problem with. Growing up without a mother hadn't helped when it came to the girlie side of things. She didn't own any makeup, and the few outfits she owned were designed for comfort, not mingling at a social event.

"Look, there's even a parking spot right in front," Violet said, sticking her arm between the seats and pointing.

"Always a good sign," Celia added.

There was nothing appealing about trying on skirts and possibly heels. Fred highly disagreed that a trip to the boutique would have a good outcome. Clamping her lips and biting back a groan, she pulled the truck into the empty spot and reluctantly let the females drag her into the store for an unwanted makeover.

CHAPTER ELEVEN

It was mid-afternoon, and still no sign of Fred and Jake's female relatives. He'd thought for sure they'd be back from town by now since Fred usually started preparations for the evening meal around that time.

Not one of the three females had called to say they were running late. He hadn't expected them to check in with him, though he'd thought for sure Fred would contact Casey, maybe even Braden, since they were now partners in managing the ranch. Asking his cousin a fourth time would most likely earn Jake more than an irritated snarl.

It hadn't helped that the day passed slowly or that he'd missed seeing Fred working the buffet table during lunch. The meal Casey and Lexi had set out was equally as good as anything Fred prepared, but the bundle of knots in his stomach kept him from enjoying it.

Jake had stayed busy by working in the barn and was putting the last saddle from the earlier trail ride back in the storage area when he heard footsteps approaching from behind him. "Hey, Noah," he said, not bothering to turn around since he'd already recognized the male's scent.

From the faded jeans, boots, and the pair of leather

gloves tucked in his back pocket, Noah was every bit the ranch hand. He preferred to keep his hair a little long, the black strands sticking out from under his tan suede cowboy hat and brushing the collar of his denim shirt.

"How was the ride?" Noah asked as he strolled further into the room.

The male was great about socializing with the guests, more because it was part of his job than anything else. Generally, when dealing with family or other staff, he didn't go out of his way to start a conversation unless he had something important to say.

Noah also took his time getting to the point. Jake had learned that no amount of prodding could get the male to share important information until he was ready. "No issues, and everyone seemed to enjoy it," Jake said, heading back to the main area of the barn that housed the stalls for the horses, knowing that Noah would follow him.

"I thought you might want to know our unexpected guest headed for town not long after the females left."

Jake hadn't anticipated an update about Conrad. It seemed everyone who lived on the property knew about his interest in Fred or that she was his mate. Noah had worked for the Walker sisters for quite a few years and always looked out for their safety. After Harlan had some of his males sneak onto the property and try to ruin Braden and Casey's wedding, Jake had been vigilant about taking a nightly run as his bear to check the grounds and the nearby forest. Jake's path had crossed with Noah's black wolf on several occasions.

"Thanks," Jake said, glad to hear that Noah had been keeping an eye on that particular guest. "I appreciate the heads up." Noah had great instincts, and his wolf must have sensed that something was off with Conrad like he had.

He wasn't offended when Noah ended the conversation with a grunt, then strolled out of the barn. If Jake was right, and Conrad's interest in Fred was more than being friendly, he didn't want him anywhere near her. Admittedly, Jake wasn't thrilled with the idea of any unmated males being around Fred.

He wanted to know if she'd seen Conrad and pulled out his phone, deliberating what he'd say to Fred when and if she answered. After their discussion the night before, any mention of the male might provoke an argument.

He could always call his mother, but shifters had exceptional hearing, and if Fred was close by, she'd be able to hear everything they talked about. Any attempts he made to make sure Fred was all right would have the same result; he'd risk alienating her again.

Frustrated, he slipped the phone back in his pocket and pushed aside his distracting thoughts, then walked the length of the aisle running between the stalls on both sides of the barn to make sure he hadn't forgotten anything. Once that was done, he crossed the compound to the lodge. Jake made it as far as the front porch when he spotted the ranch's truck pulling into the drive.

His bear wanted him to rush over to the truck as soon as Fred brought it to a stop, then pull her into his arms and hold her. He didn't understand why Jake didn't want the females to know he'd been worried or why he'd kept his strides casual as he approached the vehicle.

"How was the shopping trip?" Jake asked, shading his eyes from the glare as he peered through the passenger door window, pretending he was interested in whatever was on the back seat.

"It was fine," Fred said, nudging him away from the door so she could open it.

She was actually smiling rather than glaring at him like she usually did, so maybe he'd been worried for nothing. At least in regards to his mother and aunt. Conrad was still a mystery, but asking point-blank questions about whether or not they'd seen him might cause problems of a different nature. "Did everything go okay?"

"Of course it did," Celia said, motioning for him to move out of the way so she could take the bags Fred was holding. "Why wouldn't it?"

"Just curious," Jake said. He could think of a few reasons, most of them having to do with his mother telling Fred about all his past transgressions and how much she was looking forward to having grandbabies to spoil.

Jake was saved from being more specific by Lexi, who was strolling toward them and pushing a wheelbarrow. Emma walked beside her with one hand on the smooth metal edge, her form of helping.

"Did you get the goat food for Darla and the other goats?" Emma asked Fred.

"I sure did. It's in the back." Fred smiled as she hitched her thumb toward the truck's bed.

"Okay." Emma raced ahead, then waited for Lexi to lower the tailgate.

Violet grabbed her bags from the opposite side of the truck, then gave the surrounding area a quick glance. "Where's Braden and Casey?"

"They're in the barn cleaning out stalls." Lexi raised a brow as she hefted the bag into the wheelbarrow. "I think it's their idea of a romantic bonding experience. Personally, shoveling horse poop never did it for me in that department."

"What does do it for you?" Jake asked, realizing too late that he should've considered how Celia would react to the question.

"Well, if you must know," Lexi said, flashing a wry grin.

Lexi was like a little sister, and Jake forgot his mother hadn't been around them long enough to know that they teased each other regularly.

"No, he doesn't need to know." Fred's elbow to the ribs was unexpected, and so was the flicker of jealousy in her green eyes.

She'd never reacted that way before, at least not that

he'd noticed. He felt hopeful and invigorated at the same time. If they didn't have an audience, Jake would've pulled Fred into his arms and reassured her with a kiss. By the way everyone except Fred was trying to hide an amused grin, he didn't think they'd have a problem with a show of affection. Even Emma had a hand clamped over her mouth to stifle a giggle.

"I guess not," Jake shrugged, then walked over to his mother and slipped a finger along the opening of one of her bags to see what was inside. "What did you buy?"

"None of your business," Celia said, giving his hand a light smack and yanking the bag out of his reach. "Now scoot."

"Geez, mom," Jake stuck out his lower lip.

"Serves you right for being so nosy," Fred said, reaching behind the back seat and pulling out a Styrofoam cooler.

Jake held his hands out to Fred. "Would you like me to carry that for you?"

"No, that's okay. I've got it," Fred said.

Because the reservations followed a specific booking schedule, the guests usually left early Sunday. It gave the family and employees a night of downtime, which generally involved getting together for a meal at the house and included a frozen treat or dessert of some kind.

After spotting the cooler, Emma lost interest in helping Lexi and wiggled her way between Jake and Fred.

"You're being awfully mysterious," Jake said. "What's inside?" He took Emma's hand and paced next to Fred.

"Ice cream," Fred said, stepping around him and heading for the lodge because it had a larger refrigerator and freezing unit.

Jake hoisted Emma into his arms, then hurried to the porch so he could hold the door open for her. "You got me ice cream."

"It's for Emma." Fred sidestepped around him and headed for the kitchen.

"Yeah," Emma squealed and clapped her hands.

"You're going to share with me, right?" Jake asked Emma.

"Nope."

"But Ems, I thought I was your favorite uncle." Jake tried to look pathetic with an overexaggerated pout.

"You are," she said matter of fact after Jake placed her on her feet so she could trail after Fred.

Kelsey had arrived via the back entrance. "There you are," she said to Emma. "I thought you were helping Lexi."

"Fred got ice cream just for me." Emma looked at Jake and pursed her lips.

"I'm afraid ice cream will have to wait until after dinner."

"Aww, mom." Emma stubbornly crossed her arms and stuck out her chin. "That's not fair."

"I know." Kelsey sighed and held out her hand. "Come on, let's get you cleaned up before we eat."

"Okay." Emma shuffled her feet as she followed her mother.

"Fred, if you need any help…holler," Kelsey said.

"I've got things covered, but thanks."

Preparing a meal for the guests was no small feat, and Jake pondered Fred's parting words, trying to figure out what she meant. If Kelsey was taking care of Emma, and Casey was in the barn with Braden, and Lexi was looking after her goats, then who was helping Fred. It was almost as if everyone had disappeared on purpose, leaving Jake wondering whether or not his mother had orchestrated his time alone with Fred or if it had been his mate's idea.

Fred waited until Kelsey and Emma were gone, then faced Jake. "Since you showed such an *overbearing* interest in assisting me last night, I didn't think you'd mind helping out with the evening meal."

It appeared his mate had a sense of humor. Jake didn't miss the subtle reference to his animal and the excuse he'd used on Conrad. Fred was usually reserved when he was around. Having her open up to him like this was a promising step for their relationship, and he couldn't be happier.

Jake hadn't realized he'd been daydreaming until Fred said, "That is unless you have something else you need to be doing."

He didn't like being the cause of her furrowed brows and placed his hand over hers, enjoying the warmth of her skin and the tingle reminding him that she was his mate. It was the first time all day that he and his bear were content, that he didn't have to listen to the animal's constant growling and grumbling. If he'd let his animal have his way, they'd have shifted and traveled all the way to town to find her. "There's no place I'd rather be. What do you need me to do?"

Fred grinned, then walked across the room and grabbed two aprons off the hook mounted on the wall. One apron was a solitary dark green and the other a floral print, which she handed to him. "Things could get messy, so you'll need this."

Jake glared at the piece of extremely feminine fabric and groaned. "I don't suppose you'd let me wear that one instead, would you?"

"Sorry," Fred said, flashing him a devious grin as she finished putting on her apron. "My kitchen. My rules." She rose on her tiptoes and slipped the apron's loop over his head.

Jake secured the ties behind his back, then did a little spin. "So, does it do anything for my manly appearance?"

Fred chuckled. "I've got to have a picture." She reached into her back pocket and retrieved her cell.

Jake snatched the phone away from her before she could select the photo app, then set it on the counter out of her reach. He pulled her into his arms when she tried to snag it again. He nuzzled the side of her neck, eliciting a shudder. "You can dress me up like a female and torture me all you want," he whispered. "But there will be no pictures."

"Oh, I plan to torment you plenty." Fred pressed a gentle kiss to his lips, then stepped away. "Starting with these." She grabbed a pair of oven mitts off the counter and placed them in his hands.

Jake glared at the mitts and groaned. "Not exactly what I was hoping for."

CHAPTER TWELVE

Standing in the middle of her bedroom floor, Fred's gaze went from watching Celia, Violet, and Casey admire their handiwork to eying herself in the full-length mirror sitting in the corner. The dress Jake's mother insisted on buying her was made from a shiny emerald green fabric. It had thin shoulder straps, a slight flare from the waist to mid-thigh and fit her perfectly. Celia had also insisted that she have a pair of two-inch black heels to complete the ensemble.

Getting through her teenage years without a mother had been difficult, and she'd spent most of her time as a tomboy. Fred usually wore flats or boots and wasn't certain she'd be able to walk in the shoes that showed off her ankles without embarrassing herself.

The flutters in her stomach had to be the size of hummingbirds. The dance was only a little over an hour away. She'd never been comfortable in large crowds, and the thought of attending made her nervous. Though, deep down, she knew Jake was the underlying cause of her trepidation. He'd never seen her in a dress or wearing her long crimson curls down. What if he didn't like what he saw?

Their time spent working in the kitchen preparing the evening meal, not one day, but two in a row, had been wonderful. They'd exchanged playful banter, shared kisses when no one was looking, and had gotten much closer. Things were going well between them, so why couldn't Fred shake the feeling that something was about to go wrong.

At least she didn't have to worry about Conrad and his stalkerish behavior. According to Kelsey, he'd left right after lunch without giving her a reason why he'd checked out a day early.

"Are you sure about this?" Fred asked, not addressing anyone specifically.

"Quite sure," Celia said.

"I agree," Violet said, nodding.

In the short time they'd spent together, her respect for Celia and Violet had grown immensely, and she appreciated their help and their advice. She wouldn't, however, under any circumstances underestimate their scheming capabilities. So far, they'd done a great job of making it possible for Jake and her to get quality time together.

Fred had been reluctant when the females suggested calling Casey on the way back from town after their shopping expedition to coordinate a way for Jake to work with her in the kitchen. The sisters had been excited about helping. Even Braden, who'd also been listening to the call via speaker, had agreed with the plan.

Now that Fred had gotten to know Jake a lot more, and thanks to his mother, understood his motivations a little better, she'd taken some time to consider her own feelings. She'd been attracted to him from the moment their gazes met, yet for reasons that seemed silly now, she'd done her best to ignore him.

Fred believed in being honest and wanted their relationship to be built on trust. Jake had a right to know everything about her, so depending on how things went at the dance, she planned to tell him the truth about her past.

"What about helping Lexi?" Fred asked.

"Lexi can manage working the door by herself," Casey said.

"But what about the buffet?" Fred had a hard time relinquishing her responsibilities completely. "Who's going to take care of setting it up?"

"It's already taken care of, so stop worrying." Casey draped her arm across Fred's semi-bare shoulders. "As your boss, I expect you to take the night off because you deserve it. As your friend, I want you to go and have a great time. Right now, impressing your mate is the only task that requires your full attention."

"I think I can handle that." At least Fred hoped she could anyway. She might have felt more confident about going to the dance if the three females had allowed her to wear a pair of jeans and boots. Heck, she'd probably be better off if she didn't go at all. But not going meant not seeing Jake, and he was worth any discomfort she was experiencing.

The ranch's dances were popular with the local townsfolk, and there'd be single females attending. Besides his good looks, unlike her, Jake was at home in a social environment and would undoubtedly attract their attention. She trusted him, but it didn't mean she wanted other females hanging all over him. The stronger her emotions got, the easier it was to relate to the jealousy and uncertainty Jake must have felt when he'd seen Conrad hovering all over her.

"Of course, you can." Celia rubbed Fred's back.

"Don't forget we'll all be at the dance too, should you need us," Violet said.

Their reassuring support didn't make Fred's nervousness disappear entirely, but she no longer felt nauseous.

A mild rap had everyone looking toward the door. "Fred," Emma called from the hallway. "Can I come in?"

Casey walked over and opened the door. "Sure, sweetie. What did you need?"

Emma stepped into the room, wearing a light pink and white polka dot dress and her favorite cowboy boots. "I need someone to tie these for me?" She held up her hand to show Casey the bright pink ribbons dangling between her fingers.

"I can take care of that for you," Casey said, taking one of the ribbons and looping it around the pigtail on the left side of Emma's head.

Before she could finish tying it into a bow, Emma pulled away and rushed over to Fred. "Oooh," Emma said, petting the skirt of Fred's dress. "You are so pretty. I can't wait for Uncle Jake to see your new dress." Emma continued to move her hand up and down along the soft fabric. "He's really gonna like it."

"You think so?" Fred asked.

"Uh-huh," Emma tipped her head back and smiled up at Fred.

"Emma, why don't we finish getting ready in your room?" Casey placed her hands on the child's shoulders and aimed her toward the door. She stopped to glance at Celia and Violet. "Ladies, I assume you have this under control."

"We do," Celia said.

"Good, then we'll be going." After giving Fred a reassuring smile, Casey ushered her niece from the room, closing the door behind them.

"Now," Celia said, walking over to Fred's dresser and grabbing her brush. "Let's see what we can you about your hair."

CHAPTER THIRTEEN

"Since when do I need an escort to the dance," Jake asked as he opened the door to his room, then stepped back to let Braden enter. It wasn't like he could get lost. The short walk from the bunkhouse where he stayed to the lodge only took a few minutes.

"Since *our* mothers insisted that I make sure you look presentable and arrive on time," Braden said.

"Do you think they're up to something?" Jake asked.

Braden snorted. "When aren't they?"

"Does Casey know anything?"

"If she does, she's not talking." Braden's response held a hint of sarcasm. His cousin was happy that his mother adored his mate but was probably irked at how well they got along. Jake wouldn't be surprised if the females convinced Casey to participate in their plans. Whatever those plans might be.

Braden gave Jake an overall glance as if taking Celia's instructions seriously. "Where's your tie?"

It was a good thing the dance didn't have a dress code because Jake was never big on wearing suits. The closest he came was the nice button-down shirt and light-weight jacket he'd put on after his shower. Riding horses and working on the ranch was hard on clothes, but he did have at least one pair of jeans that looked almost like new. "It's in the back of the closet, same as yours," Jake said, after noting that his cousin had dressed in a similar fashion.

"If you're ready to go…" Braden said, reaching for the door handle.

Jake was more than ready to go to the dance and hopefully spend the rest of the evening with Fred. He'd been glancing at the clock on his nightstand every few minutes for the last hour, wishing that time would pass by faster.

Now that it was time to go, he wasn't even sure Fred would be there. The topic of the dance hadn't come up in any of the conversations he'd had with her over the last two days, so he didn't know for certain what role she'd be filling.

For years, the ranch put on a dance for its guests every Friday night. Even people from town enjoyed attending the weekly event. If Fred wasn't at the dance, then Jake planned to make a brief appearance before looking for her.

He loved to dance and had several female friends back home that counted on him to show up at the bar on the weekends to practice their moves. Nowadays, Fred was the only female he wanted to get on the floor, but she never attended the dance. She'd show up before it started, long enough to stock the snack buffet, then disappear for the rest of the evening.

Jake walked with Braden to the back of the lodge where they used the employees-only entrance to reach a room separate from the dining hall dedicated to the festivities. Quite a few people had arrived and were milling about or standing in small groups involved in conversations.

Hudson and his mate were already on the floor two-stepping to the country music playing in the background. Rick and Philip, the two eighteen-year-olds Casey paid to DJ for her every week, did a great job with music selection and handling requests.

The buffet was set up in the dining hall where there was plenty of seating. There was also a handful of small round tables and chairs placed along the outskirts of the ample dance area for those who preferred to sit and watch the activities.

Braden and Jake worked their way to the far end of the room where a separate table had been set up with ice-filled coolers containing bottled water and a variety of sodas and juices. Since the ranch catered to families, children were encouraged to attend. Many of the locals drove long distances to get home afterward. To reduce the risk of anyone operating a vehicle while intoxicated, no alcoholic beverages were served.

"Well, I'll be darned," Braden said after handing Jake a soda. "That's something I never thought I'd see."

Jake swung around to get a look at whatever had caught his cousin's attention and nearly dropped his drink. Fred was standing in the doorway wearing a thin-strapped dress that fit the contours of her petite frame perfectly. Heat surged through his entire system, but only one particular part of his body tightened, making him uncomfortably aware of how much he wanted Fred.

His gaze locked with shimmering green eyes. Fred's lips curved into a beaming smile, and at that moment, nothing and no one else in the room mattered. She was gorgeous before, but tonight she'd transformed into a goddess just for him.

"You know it's not polite to gawk," Celia said, appearing next to Jake, then using her fingertip to gently lift his dropped jaw. "Though Fred does look stunning, doesn't she?"

"Uh-huh," Jake said, refusing to end his entranced stare and break the magical spell. Most of the time, Jake resented his mother's interference in his love life, but if she had a hand in Fred's transformation, he'd make sure to thank her for it later.

Celia took Jake's drink, then patted his shoulder. "Maybe you should see to your mate before someone else does." She tipped her head toward a group of local males who were staring in Fred's direction.

Before any of them could move, Jake was across the room and standing in front of Fred. "You came." He reached for her hand. "And you look…beautiful."

"You don't look so bad yourself," Fred said, smoothing one of his lapels, lingering with her hand pressed against his chest. She took a sniff. "And you even showered off the horse smell."

"Cleaned the manure off my boots too." He lifted his leg and wiggled his foot.

She giggled. "I'm impressed."

The rest of the room finally penetrated Jake's senses. The music had slowed, and more people were headed for the floor. "Would you like to dance?"

"Sure, but I'm not very good," she said. "Your feet might take a beating."

"It doesn't matter." Jake held out his hand and led her to a place away from the other dancers. "Just follow my lead, and you'll be fine." He didn't care if she stepped on his feet all night as long as his time was spent holding her in his arms.

Fred danced a lot better than she'd admitted. She only landed on his foot once, and weighing a lot less than he did, he'd hardly noticed. Jake enjoyed seeing her eyes sparkle and hearing her laughter every time he spun her. They must have danced for almost an hour when she asked, "Would you mind if we take a break?"

"Not at all," Jake said, letting her take the lead as they left the floor. He'd caught glimpses of Braden and Casey dancing but thought it was strange that no one in the family had bothered them. It was as if everyone was purposely ensuring that they got to spend time alone together. Not that Jake was complaining. It might be selfish, but he wanted to keep Fred all to himself, to learn everything he could about her.

He paused to lean closer and ask, "What do you say we get something to drink and go sit outside?"

CHAPTER FOURTEEN

If Jake hadn't suggested going out to the patio for some privacy, Fred would have. She couldn't remember the last time she'd enjoyed herself so much, and she owed it all to Jake and her extended family. She ached to be his mate in every way possible but didn't feel right moving forward until he knew the truth about her uncle.

Miles Dawson dealt with powerful shifters, and whether Conrad worked for him or not, his arrival reminded her that she was in hiding and couldn't expect Jake to fight her battles or go on the run with her if someone came after her.

The time she'd spent with Celia and Violet had been enjoyable, but it had also been filled with guilt. There'd been a few times when she'd wanted to tell them the truth but knew she had to talk to Jake about it first. Whether she stayed or packed her bags in the morning depended on his reaction. His rejection would be unbearable, but seeing him every day and knowing they could never be together would tear her apart. Ultimately, she'd be forced to leave.

Fred was glad to see that no one else was using the patio yet. Not wanting their conversation to be heard, she walked ahead of Jake and took a seat on one of the benches sitting furthest from the doorway.

After joining her and taking a long swig of his bottled water, Jake smiled, then pushed a loose curl behind Fred's ear. "I'm glad you decided to come to the dance."

"Me too," Fred said. "That was a lot of fun... Thank you."

"It was my pleasure."

The silence between them was comfortable, though Fred knew it wouldn't last long once she shared her secret.

"My mother can get a little pushy at times," Jake said. "I hope she hasn't been too much of a pain."

"Believe it or not, Celia's been great," Fred said. "Demanding, but still great."

Jake swiped the back of his hand across his brow and blew out a relieved breath. "You don't know how glad I am to hear it."

Fred giggled. "Sweating it a little, were you?"

"Maybe." He grinned. "What about your family? Is there anything I should know before I meet them?"

Fred had never discussed her family with anyone but Casey, so she could understand why he'd be curious. The pain from losing her parents had lessened over the years, but it still caused a dull ache whenever she thought about them. An ache that quickly transformed into anger when she was reminded of her uncle and his devious plans for her future, which would now impact Jake.

She dropped her gaze to her lap and picked at the label wrapped around the center of the plastic bottle. "You won't be meeting them."

"But...why? I don't understand." He gently lifted her chin. "Is there a reason you don't want them to meet me?"

It seemed that she wasn't the only one who'd been dealing with self-doubt. Fred reached for his hand. "I couldn't have asked for a more perfect mate." She swallowed hard. "I was an only child. My mother and father passed away when I was sixteen." It had been ten years since she'd lost her parents, but talking about them was still difficult.

"I'm so sorry," Jake said, setting their drinks aside so he could hold both of her hands, his skin warm and comforting. "I can't imagine what it would be like to lose a family member, let alone two."

"Thanks, I appreciate it," Fred said, forcing a weak smile. "My life afterward wasn't so bad, more lonely than anything else."

"So, you're all alone."

"No." Fred could shake her head all she wanted, but it wouldn't make the memories of her treacherous relative go away. "I lived with my Uncle Miles for a while. He was my only living relative and was appointed as my guardian after my parents died."

When Fred had first gone to live with Miles, she'd been impressed that he was a successful businessman who owned a fancy house. Over time, her views changed. Having a nice place to call home didn't matter if the person she lived with was always busy and rarely spent time with her.

"I don't want you anywhere near him." Unable to hide her disgust, she spat out the words. "Ever."

"Did he do something to hurt you, because if he did…" Jake must've assumed Miles had caused her physical pain because he was clamping the edge of the bench as if trying to rein in his anger and his bear. Fred was confident she'd find claw marks if she looked at the wood underneath.

"It's not what you think," she said, rubbing his arm in a soothing manner, trying to calm him down.

She waited for the rigid muscles in his shoulders to relax before giving him an explanation. "Through business, my uncle deals with a lot of high-powered people, some of them shifters. I didn't work for him, but I did live with him, and it wasn't uncommon for him to ask me along when he met with investors over dinner."

Fred paused to organize her thoughts. She didn't want

to share explicit details about her life back then but would if Jake asked questions. Thankfully, he responded to her silence by massaging the back of her hand with his thumb.

"I'd never had any problems with any of my uncle's clients, but Andre Fairborn was different. There was something about him that I didn't trust." Andre was a well-known entrepreneur in the shifter world. Even though he had a charismatic personality, he'd leered at her through the entire meal, and she'd been relieved when their dinner had finally ended.

"Afterward, I told Miles how uncomfortable I'd been and tried to persuade him not to get involved with the male."

"What did your uncle say?" Jake asked.

"He told me I was imagining things and that I'd see things differently in the morning." Fred shuddered, trying not to think about how things might have turned out if she'd taken her uncle's advice and remained in her room that night. Never meeting Jake would've been at the top of the list.

"But you didn't, did you?"

"Huh-uh." Fred shifted in her seat. "Actually, I never discussed it with him again. My fox was agitated, and I couldn't get her to settle. Since I was having trouble falling asleep, I thought a warm drink might help, so I headed for the kitchen. I was halfway down the stairs when I heard my uncle talking to someone on the phone."

Fred still got nauseous every time she replayed the conversation in her head. At least she'd gotten past the point where the reminders didn't bring on unwanted tears. "He hadn't mentioned Andre by name, but I knew he was talking to him because he asked what he thought about me, then a few seconds later told him he was happy they had a deal and that he'd enjoy having me as his new mate."

"But you can't be his mate because you're mine," Jake said, his voice filled with anger and deeper than normal because of his bear.

Fred cringed. "Apparently, that didn't matter to either of them."

"Did you confront him about it?" Jake asked.

"No, I knew if I didn't leave right away, I'd be trapped forever. I snuck back to my room and stuffed whatever I could fit into my travel bag, then dropped it behind the bushes outside my window so I could collect it in the morning. Instead of going to work like I normally did, I went to the bank and cleaned out what little money I had in my accounts and took the first available bus out of town."

"Is that how you ended up at the ranch?" Jake asked.

"Not at first," Fred said. "I was afraid my uncle would send someone after me, so I moved around quite a bit. While I was on the run, I accessed some shifter-only sites online and discovered that Miles had made some bad investments, and his business was in trouble. I also found out that Andre didn't have a spotless reputation. He was involved in loaning money."

"Do you think your uncle borrowed from Andre?" Jake asked.

"Yes, and I think he was going to use me to pay him back." She searched Jake's expression, looking for any signs that he planned to walk away. When Fred didn't see any, she continued, "When Conrad showed up, I worried that he might be working for Miles, and I'd have to go on the run again. Since he's gone, I'm glad I was wrong."

"Even if you'd been right, and Conrad did work for your uncle, this is your home," Jake said. "There's no way I'm letting you leave or giving him a chance to get anywhere near you." He pulled her onto his lap. "Have you told anyone else about this?"

"Only Casey."

"Then I think it's time *we* tell everyone. They're not going to let you leave anymore than I am, and there's safety in numbers."

Fred was relieved that Jake hadn't rejected her, but she

was still concerned about everyone else. "I don't want my being here to turn everyone's life upside down."

"I can think of one way to make the problem go away," Jake said, running his finger underneath her dress strap, eliciting a shudder.

"Jake, I don't want you to claim me just to make sure no one else can. Especially if it's not what you want."

He groaned. "You're kidding, right? I've wanted to put my mark on your lovely shoulder ever since the day I tasted your fried chicken."

"Oh, so you're saying it's my cooking you're after."

"Among other things." He wrapped his arms around her waist, pulling her closer. His hardened shaft pressing against her thigh left no doubts as to what other things he was talking about. Starting at the crook of her neck, he placed soft kisses on her skin until he reached her mouth and captured her lips. The kiss went from gentle to possessive, involved a mingling of tongues, and left them both panting.

"I'd really like to show you my room," Jake rasped, letting her know he was serious about his proposal. "Unless you'd like to stay and do some more dancing."

"No, but I have a better idea," Fred said, sliding from his lap, then taking his hand. "Come with me." Rather than go back inside, she led him toward the opposite side of the building and stopped when they reached the barn where Lexi kept her animals.

"What do you think?" she glanced over at him, hoping he'd be open to the idea of making love in the rafters.

"We definitely won't have to worry about anyone interrupting us, but are you sure Darla won't mind?"

Fred gave his arm a light smack on her way inside. "I'm pretty sure she'll be okay sharing the barn with us for one night." As she walked by the pens, she checked to make sure the animals were still sleeping. With Darla's habit of escaping, the last thing they needed was for any of them to get out.

"Wait a second," Jake whispered, then dashed to the storage room. He returned a minute later with a couple of blankets, then responded to Fred's raised brow by saying, "Hey, they might smell like the barn, but they're clean, and you won't have to worry about the straw ending up in places it shouldn't."

"You're so thoughtful." Fred reached for the rung on the ladder leading to the loft above. Halfway to the top, she could feel the heat from Jake's breath on her ankle and stopped to glance down at him. "Are you looking under my dress?"

"I am a male, and you should've let me go first if you didn't want me checking out you're lovely…backside." He smirked up at her. "Besides, I didn't think it would matter since you're not going to be wearing it much longer anyway."

Fred remembered Celia's comments about her mate's passionate side and wondered if Jake took after his father or if he was the complete opposite. She suppressed a giggle and said, "How romantic."

He tucked the blankets under the arm gripping the ladder, then skimmed the back of her leg. "I didn't say I wasn't going to take my time."

Fred's body heated. At this rate, they were never going to make it to the loft. The idea of making out while clinging to the ladder got her moving again.

When they reached the top, Fred walked over to the far wall, opened the small double doors, and stood near the opening to enjoy the cool evening breeze. The music filtering through the air from the lodge, coupled with a clear view of the forest and the night sky as a backdrop, provided an enchanting ambiance.

Lexi's goats loved to climb on things, including any hay or straw they could access, so she stored the extra bales she used for bedding in the pens below in a corner on the wooden floor. Jake hoisted a bale off the stack, then pulled out a pocket knife to cut the twine used to keep it together. After forming a nice layer on the floorboards, he spread a blanket and joined her.

He looped his arm around her waist and pulled her back to lean against his chest. "You really are beautiful," he said as he pushed aside her hair and pressed his lips to her shoulder.

Fred closed her eyes, savoring his nearness, the warmth of his body, and the enticing tingles that she could only get from her true mate.

"This is where I plan to leave my mark," Jake said, grazing her skin with his teeth.

She shivered, her body heating. "Is that so?" she asked as she turned in his arms and placed her palms on his chest.

"Uh-huh," he said. "But there are a few other things I need to do first, starting with removing this." He reached behind her and pulled down her zipper, then slowly slipped the straps from her shoulders, making sure to brush his fingertips across her skin as he went. He hadn't been kidding about extending the process of removing her clothes. By the time her dress and panties dropped to the floor, her entire body was on fire.

"Much better," Jake said, taking a moment to admire her naked body as if he'd finally found the one thing he'd been searching for his whole life. Afterward, he scooped her into his arms and gently placed her on their makeshift bed. It wasn't exactly comfortable, but he'd packed enough straw under the blanket to keep her from feeling the stiff board underneath.

Jake pushed to his feet, then undid the top button on his shirt. "Would you like it fast or slow?"

What she wanted was his naked body pressed against hers, then they could discuss the fast or slow thing. But if Jake was willing to give her a show, she wasn't about to deny herself an exquisite performance. Fred propped on her elbows so she could see every inch of him. "Slow, definitely slow."

Jake grinned and took his time with the remaining buttons, his firm muscles rippling as he slipped the fabric from his body. The male was truly put together in all the right places. He held her gaze the entire time, the intensity making her hotter with each passing second.

Fred was enjoying the show, but she reached the last of her patience when he unfastened the buckle on his pants and began lowering his zipper…way too slowly. "I changed my mind," she said, pushing off the blanket and replacing his hands with hers.

"Okay, then," Jake chuckled and held his arms out to the side, letting her remove the rest of his clothes in an expedient manner.

The instant she finished, he pulled her close, his lips aggressively capturing hers. It seemed that Fred wasn't the only one whose control had been pushed to the limit. When he lifted her off the ground, she wrapped her legs around his waist, his rigid shaft pressing the sensitive area between her thighs, drawing out a moan.

He made his way back to the blanket and gently laid Fred on her back, his mouth never leaving hers. Though they were both panting by the time their lips parted, he continued pressing tantalizing kisses to the skin along her neck, working his way down until he'd found her breast and sucked the nipple into his mouth.

The way he worked the tip into a hardened bud with his tongue had Fred whimpering and gripping his shoulders. The ache between her legs had reached an unbearable level, and she wanted him inside her. "Jake, I need you," she said, wiggling her hips.

"I know," he said, his tone smug as he moved on to her other breast, giving it the same attention as the first.

Not one to be ignored or cater to a male shifter's dominant side, Fred reached between them, determined to get what she wanted.

"So demanding," Jake teased as he pinned her hands above her head, then aligned his shaft, stopping after the first powerful thrust. "Is this what you had in mind?"

"Yes, but if you stop, I swear it will be a long time before I make you any more of my chicken."

"Well, we can't have that," Jake chuckled, then started moving, driving in and out at a steady pace that pushed her towards the edge of ecstasy. Sensing that she was close, he released her hands and paused to study her face. "Are you sure you're ready?"

He didn't have to be specific for her to know he was talking about claiming. The coveted mark would be permanent. There was no going back once he bit her. They'd be bonded forever. She appreciated his thoughtfulness in allowing her to set the pace, but more than anything, Fred wanted him to bite her, well, that and to do some biting of her own. The thought of showing off the scar and letting the rest of the shifter community know that she'd found her mate was exhilarating.

"I've never been more ready," Fred said, baring her neck to him.

The initial piercing of her skin was painful but quickly turned to pleasure, which intensified the more Jake pushed into her. Wanting him to enjoy the same experience, she brushed several kisses along his shoulder, then clamped down on the firm muscle. Jake shuddered as they both reached their orgasm together, then collapsed on top of her, gasping.

When his breathing finally evened, he rolled to the side, pulling her with him, then covering their bodies with the other blanket. "Fred," he said, tucking her hair behind her ear.

"Yeah," she mumbled, content and on the verge of succumbing to sleep.

"You were only kidding about the chicken, right?"

CHAPTER FIFTEEN

Fred had never needed an alarm because her internal clock ensured that she woke up at the right time every day. Grainger crowing in the distance along with the sun's rays slipping through the small door of the barn's loft confirmed that she hadn't overslept.

She could hear the animals stirring in the pens beneath them. It wouldn't be long before they started making noises to let anyone within earshot know they were hungry. Darla was usually the loudest, and once she got started, the rest of the mismatched herd would join her.

The thin blanket draped over Jake and her didn't provide much protection from the chill in the early morning air. A shifter's body naturally generated more heat, even in human form, but it didn't stop her from snuggling closer to Jake's naked form.

The time they'd spent pleasuring each other was longer than the time they'd spent sleeping. Even so, Fred couldn't believe how alert and well-rested she felt or elated that she and Jake were officially mated, bonded in a way that pulled them closer together and would last for the rest of their lives.

She touched the mark on her shoulder and smiled. The

spot was tender but already healing. She couldn't wait to see what it looked like in a mirror and show it off to her friends.

If Fred wasn't responsible for providing breakfast for the guests, she would've gladly spent the remainder of the morning there with Jake. Or at least whatever time she had before Lexi came out to take care of the animals.

"I'm going for coffee," Fred whispered in Jake's ear. "I'll be right back."

"No, stay here," Jake mumbled and tightened the arm he had wrapped around her waist. Fred already knew he wasn't a morning person and wasn't surprised that he hadn't opened his eyes or that it looked like he'd gone back to sleep.

"I've got to go," she said, giggling at his attempt to keep her from escaping when she wiggled free from his grasp.

After sifting through the pile of clothes, she slipped on her panties. Instead of wearing her dress, which would involve messing with the zipper, she put on Jake's shirt, taking a moment to enjoy his scent before fastening the buttons.

Satisfied that she was decently covered, Fred knelt down next to Jake, smiling at how peaceful he looked, and pressed a kiss to his forehead. Because of her fox, the pads of her feet were conditioned to endure the elements, and going barefoot was preferable to wearing fancy heels. It also made climbing down the ladder much easier.

Fred crept past the pens, being as quiet as possible and making sure to stay out of Darla's line of sight. Once she reached the opening to the barn, she peeked outside and craned her neck, listening for any signs of movement. Shifters weren't bothered by the lack of clothing on others, but some of the guests were human and might not be okay with what she was currently wearing.

Convinced that she was alone, Fred hurried toward to lodge and the path running beside it. The sisters had a habit of sleeping in a little later on the weekends, so there was a good chance she'd make it to her room without running into anyone. If she didn't dally, she'd be able to change clothes and take Jake a cup of coffee before she had to prepare breakfast for the guests.

***

Conrad had just found a spot to park his jeep when his cell phone played a musical tune. After seeing Miles Dawson's name on the screen, he took a few seconds to tamp down his frustration before answering the call.

He didn't get a chance to speak before Miles barked, "Why is it taking you so long to do your job?" The male was Conrad's current employer, the most annoying person he'd ever worked for, and a major pain in his backside. "You were supposed to bring her to me two days ago."

The 'her' the male referred to was his niece Fredericka Dawson. Conrad had been thrilled when he'd found her staying at the Crescent Canyon Ranch. Fred was the name she went by, and locating her had been difficult but not impossible. If she'd continued to move around, instead of making the place her home, he might still be trying to track her down.

Conrad scowled and held the cell phone away from his ear. Being part wolf came with enhanced hearing. He could've held the phone two feet away and still been able to hear the male rant.

Miles arriving in Waynesrock unexpectedly the day before, rather than wait for Conrad to deliver Fred to his home in California, only added to his irritation.

Once Conrad was certain Miles had finished complaining, he returned the phone to his ear. Straining to keep his voice calm, he said, "Like I explained to you before, your niece has a close relationship with the females who own the ranch, and she spends a lot of time with them. I can't walk into the place and force her to leave without drawing unnecessary attention."

Especially not with the two male bears and wolf they had on staff, treating him suspiciously and watching everything he did. Or the older females who spent a lot of time with Fred, keeping an eye on her as if she were their own cub.

Conrad's clients paid well and expected discreet service. He only asked questions pertinent to acquiring whatever he'd been tasked to find. Guilt wasn't an emotion he experienced often. On retrieval cases like this one, he didn't ask what would happen to the person after they'd been returned. He enjoyed his job and didn't lose sleep over the things he was tasked to do, not when it kept plenty of money in the bank, allowed him to do what he wanted, and travel anywhere he chose.

Conrad might be overconfident at times, but he wasn't stupid. Human laws didn't always apply when it came to the shifter community. The ranch owners and their employees were like a family. Any attempt to take Fred before he had a good escape plan in place could mean an end to his life. With the ranch being out in the middle of nowhere, hiding his body where no one would find it wouldn't be a problem.

Being under constant scrutiny was the reason he'd checked out a day early. Conrad hoped by making everyone think he'd left town, they wouldn't be so protective, and he'd have a better chance of getting to Fred when she was alone.

"Well, you're running out of time," Miles snarled.

Tired of arguing with the male, Conrad said, "You'll have your niece today", then disconnected the call.

While he was still at the ranch, Conrad took a long walk to scout the forest area bordering the property. He'd found an old dirt road that connected with the main highway leading into Waynesrock. The road was rutted and overgrown with grass and weeds in several places, making driving difficult, but nothing the four-wheel-drive in his jeep couldn't handle.

Seeing in the dark wasn't a problem, so he'd arrived before dawn to make the trek to the ranch. It was a long walk and would've gone a lot faster if he'd transformed into his wolf. To get Fred to his vehicle, however, he'd need to remain in human form. Some of the guests liked to explore the forest, so he'd dressed himself to look like a hiker by wearing comfortable boots and carrying a backpack. The disguise might help him get on the property, but it wouldn't do much good if he was seen after he grabbed Fred.

After confirming Fred's identity, finding easy access to the ranch wasn't the only reason he'd decided to stay. Conrad also needed to document Fred's daily routine. Stopping by the garden to pick vegetables was the first thing she did every morning before heading to the lodge. The large patch was located behind the building and near the forest's edge. He'd decided it was the best place to take her without anyone noticing.

Conrad arrived in the area around the same time the sun lit up the sky with pinks and yellows. Not long after the rooster finished crowing, he heard a female humming. The sound was coming from the direction of the smaller of several barns instead of the house where the owners lived. He hadn't expected anyone to be out here this early and pressed closer to the rear wall of the lodge so he wouldn't be seen.

He couldn't believe his luck when Fred came into view. Her legs and feet were bare. The only thing covering her body was an overly large male shirt that reached the middle of her thighs. The crimson strands draping her shoulders were in a mussed state, and if he wasn't mistaken, there were a few pieces of straw stuck to the back of her head.

After inhaling deeply to catch a scent, it was obvious she'd spent the night in the barn with Jake. It wasn't a surprise since the male had made his intentions about the female clear the night he'd challenged him at the buffet table.

At the time, Conrad hadn't noticed a claiming mark or smelled the male's scent on her body, so he didn't know if she was his mate. A shifter could go their whole life without finding their match. It didn't mean they preferred a solitary existence or that they wouldn't choose to share their lives with someone else.

Jake being Fred's mate would make things a lot more complicated, and he risked having the male hunt him down to get her back. If Miles hadn't agreed to pay him three times his regular fee, Conrad would've waited for her to go inside the house, then walked away.

Greed was an excellent motivator, and Conrad figured the sooner he snatched Fred and turned her over to Miles, the sooner he could collect his money, and the bear would become the other male's problem.

***

Fred had been so focused on getting to the house unnoticed so she could return to Jake that she hadn't caught Conrad's scent until it was too late. She didn't even get a chance to scream before he had her arms pinned to her sides and his hand clamped over her mouth.

Struggling against a much bigger male who possessed the additional strength of a wolf was futile, but it didn't stop Fred from trying. "Stop squirming, or this is going to be painful," Conrad said, then squeezed her arm until she winced. "I'd hate to turn you over to your uncle covered in bruises, but I will if I have to."

She didn't doubt that he'd follow through on his threat and immediately stopped fighting. Bruises she could handle. It was being rendered unconscious that she was unwilling to risk. She had no idea if Conrad had to take her all the way to California or if Miles was staying close by. What if Conrad hadn't been looking for her the day she'd seen him in town but had gone to meet her uncle?

Fred had been gone for months, and Miles had to be desperate. He wasn't a patient man, so assuming he'd arrived in Wyoming was easy, which meant she needed to find a way to escape before Conrad took her off the property.

"Good girl," he said smugly, then started walking, her feet dangling because he'd lifted her off the ground. Getting to the forest would've been faster if he'd gone past the house, but Fred assumed he wanted to leave without being seen.

Other than Jake, who'd been asleep when she left the barn, no one knew she was out here and wouldn't realize she was missing until long after she was gone. The thought of never seeing Jake or her friends again brought moisture to her eyes, but as hopeless as things seemed, she wasn't going to give up. Nor was she going to give Conrad the satisfaction of making her cry. She blinked to stop any tears and concentrated on her surroundings.

A distraction would be nice. Something to get him to loosen his grip so she could shift. Sadly, there wasn't anything in the area that would help. By the time they'd reached the chicken coop, Fred's body ached from the way Conrad had carried her. She was almost ready to give up hope until she saw Grainger...outside the coop.

For once, Fred was glad that Lexi hadn't repaired the building to keep the chickens from escaping. She was even happier knowing that Grainger didn't like strangers. And Conrad was no exception. As soon as the bird spotted the male, he squawked and flapped his wings. Knowing the intimidating threat was a precursor for an attack, she counted on the feathered fowl to provide the help she needed.

The two hens who'd gotten out with Grainger were also moving around, clucking and making distressed noises.

Any other time, seeing the bird ruffle his feathers and

sprint on short legs across the ground would've been comical if she wasn't the victim of a kidnapping. Conrad acted as if the birds' display wasn't important, a mistake he realized a few seconds later when Grainger ran up to him and started attacking his leg with his beak.

"What the…" Conrad snarled, lashing out with his foot, which agitated the rooster even more. He flapped his wings and lifted off the ground, going after Conrad's legs again with his sharp claws.

In his rush to move out of the way, his hand slipped off Fred's mouth, and she didn't hesitate to sink her teeth into his soft flesh until she tasted blood. He growled, pulling his hand away from her mouth and loosening his grip around her chest.

Able to work an arm free, Fred elbowed him in the ribs as hard as she could, then tucked her legs and kicked him above the knees, using the momentum to push out of his arms entirely. As soon as she landed on the ground, she shifted and screamed with her animal's voice hoping someone would hear her, that Jake would come to her rescue.

"Damn it," Conrad swore, and a few seconds later, the sound of fabric tearing echoed through the air.

Fred's fox couldn't outrun the wolf for long, but maybe she'd get lucky and find a hole or space large enough to hide in until help arrived. After shrugging off the remnants of Jake's shirt, she skidded around the corner of the coop and ran in the general direction of the barns. If Conrad caught her again, there'd be no escaping from him a second time.

Fred's fox made it as far as the corral outside the horse barn when Conrad's wolf caught up to her. As soon as he pounced, she burrowed under the lowest board of the fence, barely escaping, but not before he grazed her hind leg with his claws.

Yelping, she scrambled toward the barn. Her leg throbbed, and she scented her own blood. She didn't have time to stop and see how badly she'd been injured. The gaps between the boards were too narrow for the wolf to fit through, but it wouldn't stop him from jumping over the fence.

There was nowhere left to run that he wouldn't be able to catch her. The best she could do was crawl in with one of the horses and try to defend herself.

CHAPTER SIXTEEN

Darla and the handful of other goats whose names Jake couldn't remember must be hungry because their bleating was growing increasingly louder and had reached a point where he couldn't ignore them anymore. He slowly opened his eyes to find that the spot under the blanket next to him no longer held any warmth. He'd been so content and relaxed that he'd fallen back asleep after Fred told him she was going for coffee. Now that he was awake, he realized she'd been gone a long time.

Females liked to chat. It was possible she'd gotten delayed by one of the sisters or his mother and aunt. If he didn't have an overwhelming sense of dread urging him to find her, he wouldn't have given it much thought.

He tossed aside the blanket and reached for his pants, noticing that Fred's dress was where it had fallen the night before, but his shirt was missing. The joy he'd felt after noticing that she'd chosen to wear his clothes instead of hers disintegrated the instant he heard her fox's distressed plea for help.

Jake discarded his pants and dove through the loft's doorway, transforming into his bear, his four paws hitting hard on the ground below. The guest cabins were on the other side of the compound, but even if they weren't, he didn't care that his bear might frighten those that were human.

All he cared about was getting to his mate. He didn't know what kind of trouble Fred was in, but after what she'd shared about her uncle and her concerns about Conrad, he was sure he had a good idea.

He ran in the direction of Fred's scream, skidding as he rounded the back of the lodge. The rooster and hens were milling about in the garden and scattered at the sight of his bear. Jake picked up Fred's scent intermingled with Conrad's, then wished he'd been more vigilant in his nightly patrols of the ranch. Checking out and leaving the property had been a clever tactic, and Jake cursed himself for falling for it.

Now that he had Fred's scent, he continued following it, then stopped when he reached the area near the chicken coop and found what was left of his shirt, the wolf's shredded clothes, and a backpack. It appeared as if the male had tried to snatch Fred, and she'd shifted to escape. It would explain why the scream he'd heard had been made by her animal.

Just as Jake was pressing his snout to the ground to pick up Fred's scent again, Braden arrived, a pair of sweat pants the only thing he was wearing. "Jake, what's wrong?"

If Jake was right about Conrad's intentions, then he'd also transformed to go after her. In her fox form, she wouldn't be able to evade the wolf for very long. His mate needed him, and Jake didn't have time to shift back into his human form so he could explain what had happened. He responded to his cousin with a growl and pawed the pile of torn clothes.

Braden hurried over, picked up a piece of fabric to smell, then growled. "Conrad."

Casey sprinted up behind them, a frantic expression on her face. If they weren't in the middle of a dire situation, Jake would have teased her about the messed-up state of her hair and the animal slippers on her feet. "Braden, what's going on?" she asked. "Why is Jake a bear?" She saw the torn clothes. "Did something happen to Fred?"

"I'll take care of this. You go find your mate," Braden ordered. "I'll be right behind you."

In the past, no matter what they'd encountered, they'd always been there for each other. Jake appreciated his cousin's support, but dealing with Conrad was something he planned to handle alone.

He hurried in the direction Fred had gone, hoping with every heavy pad of his paw that she'd be okay when he found her. Because if Conrad had done anything to hurt his mate, the male would be leaving the place in pieces. If he left at all.

Fred's trail led Jake to the corral attached to the horse barn. He found a spot where she'd slipped under the fence. The scent of fresh blood lingering in the air, as well as the drops spotting the dried earth on the other side of the fence, enraged him and his bear. It took all his willpower to stop the animal from tearing through the wooden boards instead of going around them.

When he entered the barn, he found Conrad naked and standing near the partially open gate of Belle's stall. The male held a lead rope in his hand and was trying to slip it over Belle's head. The horse didn't want anything to do with him, nor did she want him in her pen. By the way she was shaking her head and pawing the dirt, Jake wondered if Fred was inside and the mare was trying to protect her.

He released a warning roar, then barreled toward Conrad, who dropped the lead and shifted into his wolf seconds before Jake could reach him. The crafty wolf dodged the attack by diving to the right and springing off the half-wall separating the pens on the opposite side of the center aisle.

Fred's fox appeared next to Belle, then barked to let Jake know she was all right. He would've chased after Conrad, who'd bolted for the open doorway at the other end of the barn, if Braden, in the form of his bear, hadn't appeared and stopped him.

Fred walked toward Jake, her progress hindered by a subtle limp on her rear leg. Seeing the blood-crusted fur was Jake's undoing. He rushed Conrad, pinning the wolf to the ground with his jaw clamped on the animal's neck. The urge to snap his neck, which wouldn't take much effort, was overwhelming.

"Jake, don't. He's not worth it," Fred said. She'd transformed and pressed her body against his side, sinking her fingers into his fur, the contact calming his bear.

Slowly, the need to hurt the male subsided, and Jake released the wolf. Braden moved closer and grunted, letting Jake know that he'd make sure Conrad didn't go anywhere. He shifted and pulled Fred into arms, unwilling to let her go.

***

Fred clung to Jake's shaking body, giving him the time he needed to calm down completely. As much as she wanted Conrad to pay for what he'd done or tried to do, she didn't want her mate to live with the guilt of taking his life. Besides, the real culprit was her uncle, and if he was in town as she'd suspected, she needed Conrad's help to locate him.

Fred hoped she wouldn't have to go back to California but personally wanted to make sure the despicable male knew she was mated and didn't send anyone else to find her.

When Jake finally released her, he ran his hands along her body, stopping when he reached the wound on her leg. "Are you all right?"

"The cut's not bad, and it's already healing," Fred said, glancing down at her sore limb.

Casey appeared carrying a stack of blankets. She handed one to Fred and kept her gaze averted as she gave another one to Jake. Turning her attention to Conrad, she said, "Shift back, and if you try to escape, I'll have my mate remove a few body parts."

It didn't take much guesswork for Fred to know what part of the male anatomy Casey had in mind. Conrad must have figured it out as well because he immediately complied. After tossing a blanket on the ground next to the male, Casey stepped around him to hand the last one to Braden, who'd already returned to his human form.

"Fred, why don't you come with me back to the house so I can take a look at your leg," Casey said.

"I'm not leaving until Conrad tells me where I can find my uncle." She glared at the male because he was taking his time getting to his feet and wrapping the towel around his hips.

"Why would I do that?" Conrad sneered.

"Mostly so I don't let my mate finish what he started," Fred said.

Before Conrad could answer, Hudson and Mallory entered the barn through the entryway Braden had been guarding. Celia and Violet appeared a few seconds later.

"Is everyone all right?" Celia asked, her gaze drawn to Fred, no doubt because she'd scented her blood.

After all the noise her fox had made, Fred had expected more of the ranch's guests to show up.

"You know, back in the day, we knew how to take care of deplorable males like him. I'd be happy to help out," Hudson said, reaching for the tie securing his bathrobe.

Mallory frowned and put her hand over his. "We're on our honeymoon. There will be no fighting. Not if you want to enjoy any more of our alone time."

"But…" he groaned.

"I mean it." Mallory crossed her arms and tapped her foot.

"Sorry, boys. It looks like you're on your own," he groaned, then took his mate's hand and started to leave.

"Actually, there is something you can do to help,"

Casey said.

Hudson stopped and gave her a hopeful grin. "Name it."

"Could you let the rest of the guests know that breakfast is going to be a little late this morning?"

He slumped his shoulders. "Sure, I can do that."

"If you want, Violet and I can handle the buffet for you," Celia said.

"Are you sure?" Casey asked.

Violet tsked. "Absolutely."

Just as the two females were leaving, Lexi marched into the barn, carrying her deceased father's shotgun. "What did I miss?" She spotted Conrad and said, "Oh, never mind."

Fred began to worry when Kelsey showed up alone a few seconds later. "Where's Emma," she asked. Kelsey never left her daughter unattended, and she wanted to make sure the child was in a safe place and unable to hear their conversation.

"She's in the house with Noah," Kelsey said, her gaze jumping to Lexi. "You need to put that thing away."

"Why?" Lexi gripped the weapon tighter as if Kelsey might try to wrestle it away from her.

"Because I called the Waynesrock police department, and they're sending out a deputy to take care of him." Kelsey pointed at Conrad.

"It's lucky for you that my sister has a kind heart and decided to turn you over to local law enforcement; otherwise, we'd be digging *another* grave up on the mountain," Casey said, her tone serious. Fred knew she was kidding, but Conrad seemed uncertain and grimaced.

"Now that we've got your attention," Fred said. "How about giving me that information I wanted."

CHAPTER SEVENTEEN

According to Conrad, Miles was staying at the only hotel in Waynesrock. For how much longer, he didn't know. Per their arrangements, Conrad was supposed to deliver Fred to him before the end of the day. It took Fred, with Braden's help, to restrain Jake after he heard that tidbit of information.

Fred couldn't blame her mate for being upset. After Conrad's kidnapping attempt and the injury to her leg, she wasn't happy with the wolf either. Her fox agreed with Jake and would've gladly helped with any altercations he wanted to inflict on the male.

During a group meeting, which involved everyone, less Emma and Noah, cramming into the house kitchen, it was decided that Fred and Jake would drive into town to confront Miles. It had taken quite a bit of convincing to get the rest of the females to remain behind.

She'd expected Lexi and Kelsey to be upset with her after finding out she'd kept her secret from them. It had warmed Fred to the core when all three sisters pulled her into a group hug and told her she was family and there was no way they were letting her leave.

Fred climbed the stairs to the second-floor landing.

Her heart was beating so loud and fast that her ears were ringing. Part of her dreaded the upcoming confrontation. The other part wanted it over with, so she wouldn't have to deal with Miles ever again. "It must be the room on the end up there," she said to Jake once they'd reached the halfway point of the narrow walkway.

Thoughts of what she'd say to the male after all this time had raced through her mind the entire drive into town. Now that she'd reached her destination, the mentally rehearsed words escaped her.

Jake sensed her distress and gave her arm a gentle tug to pull her to a stop. "It's all right if you'd rather wait in the truck and let me handle him."

"I appreciate it, but after everything he's done, I need to do this."

"I'll support whatever you want to do," Jake said, flexing his fingers, a mock demonstration of his bear's claws and teeth, which would be way more effective than those of her fox.

"Thanks, but we agreed there'd be no bloodshed, remember?" Something Fred's animal disagreed with and was still miffed about because her opinion had been ignored.

Jake shrugged. "Just thought I'd throw it out there in case you changed your mind."

"Thanks," Fred said, still amazed at how a few supportive words from her mate helped her relax and gave her the confidence she needed to face anything.

After taking a long calming breath, she double-checked the number on the door, then gave it several raps.

"It's about time," Miles said as he yanked the door open, then froze.

"Hello, Miles." Fred wasn't one to gloat but beamed with satisfaction when her uncle's face paled, and his angry expression faded to shock as soon as he saw Jake standing behind her.

"Fred," he said, nervously leaning forward to peer

along the walkway, no doubt looking for Conrad. "What are you doing here?" He did a terrible job of sounding bewildered. They both knew he'd been expecting her arrival, even if it hadn't been voluntary.

"I'd ask you the same thing if I didn't already know the answer," she said, pinning him with a disgusted glare. It had been months since she'd seen her uncle last, yet he looked like he'd aged several years. There was an abundance of gray streaks in his dark hair, and the skin beneath his eyes was shadowed, the surrounding wrinkles more pronounced than she remembered.

"I don't know what you mean," Miles stammered.

"Sure you do," Fred said. "That's why you were looking for Conrad, but I'm afraid he won't be coming. He's currently at the police station explaining why he tried to kidnap me and giving them all your information." She didn't know if the last part was true, but she was okay with Miles believing it was.

She glanced at Jake, impressed that he'd remained composed and let her handle things. She wasn't sure she'd be able to do the same if roles were reversed and someone had tried to take him from her.

"Then why did you bother coming here?" Miles asked.

"First, to let you know that I will never let you force me into a mating I don't want." Her uncle's face turned red, so Fred held up her hand to keep him from arguing. "And second, I wanted you to meet my *true* mate." She leaned into Jake after he slipped his arm behind her back.

"That's not possible," Miles grumbled.

"It truly is, and I can prove it." Fred tugged on the collar of her shirt to expose the claiming mark.

"Fred, you have to understand. My business was in trouble, and I was about to lose everything, including our home."

Groveling wasn't a good look for her uncle, and she didn't want to hear an apology, though she had doubts he'd ever give her one. But if he did, it wouldn't be sincere.

"No," Fred said through gritted teeth, then poked him in the chest. "It was your home, not mine. And if you were any kind of family, you wouldn't have tried to use me to settle your debt. But, hey, if you leave now, you might make it out of town before the police start looking for you. Though, I'm not sure going back home will be much better, not after Andre finds out you can't repay him."

"Fred," Miles said, reaching for her arm, then snatching his hand away when Jake took an imposing step forward.

"Just so we're clear," Jake snarled. "If you or any of your hired goons come anywhere near my mate again, there won't be enough left of you to make a fur hat."

***

Jake had been proud of the way Fred dealt with her uncle. After everything she'd been through, he was also worried about her emotional state. No one went through life without experiencing some form of betrayal, but what Miles had done to Fred had to be tearing her up inside.

She hadn't spoken much during the drive back to the ranch. Most of her time was spent staring out the passenger door window. She'd been so quiet that Jake continually glanced in her direction to make sure she was okay.

Pushing her to talk about what happened wouldn't do any good until she was ready. In fact, it could possibly make things worse.

He'd been pondering a way to take her mind off things and came up with an idea right before they'd reached the ranch. "Fred, would you mind taking a walk with me?" he asked as he parked the truck. "I have something I want to show you."

"Sure, but don't you think we should check in first and let everyone know we're back?" she asked.

"It won't take long...promise." He jumped out of the vehicle and raced around to her side before opening the door. "But you have to keep your eyes closed until I tell you it's okay to look."

"Jake." She narrowed her green gaze. "What are you up to?"

"You'll see." He grinned.

Once she closed her eyes, he took her hand. "No peeking either," he said, then led her to the place he'd hidden the supplies he'd gathered for the greenhouse. He'd planned to wait a few more days to give her time to adjust to being mated before giving her the gift but now seemed like the right time.

"Can I look yet?" Fred asked as soon as they stopped.

"Just a second." Jake stepped behind her, then slipped his arms around her waist and pulled her back against his chest.

"Okay, you can open your eyes."

Fred stared at the stack of wood for several seconds, then asked, "Am I supposed to guess?"

"I know it doesn't look like much now, but it's going to be a greenhouse once you tell me where you want it," he said.

For the longest time, she didn't say anything, and Jake wondered if he'd been wrong in his choice of gifts. "If you don't like it, I can get you something else."

"No." She twisted in his arms to face him. "Don't you dare." A tear slipped down her cheek, and she hurried to wipe it away. "It's absolutely wonderful, and I know right where I want you to build it." She reached up and pulled his head forward, pressing her lips against his, the tantalizing kiss, long and filled with passion.

If she was this excited about the greenhouse, he wondered how she would react when he told her about his plans for a cabin. With Braden already living in the house with Casey, he thought it might get a little crowded with him sharing Fred's room. He didn't think moving into the bunkhouse would be fair to Noah, so he figured he'd talk to the rest of the family about building a small place of their own.

"Whatcha guys doing?" Hearing Emma's voice caused them to pull apart.

"Jake was showing me the stuff he got for the greenhouse he's going to make me," Fred said.

"No, you weren't." Emma rolled her eyes. "You were kissing."

"What are you doing out here?" Jake asked, trying to change the subject.

"Mom sent me to tell you it's time for ice cream."

"Does that mean you're going to share some of yours with me?" Jake asked.

"Nooo," Emma said, then took off running.

"I'm not sharing mine with you either," Fred giggled, then hurried after Emma.

"But you're my mate. Doesn't that mean you're supposed to share everything with me?"

"I don't think so," she yelled back at him.

Jake chased the females back to the house, grinning all the way. He'd finally found the perfect female and didn't think life could get any better...well, not unless he and Fred had a few little ones of their own.

* * *

ABOUT THE AUTHOR

Rayna Tyler is an author of paranormal and sci-fi romance. She loves writing about strong sexy heroes and the sassy heroines who turn their lives upside down. Whether it's in outer space or in a supernatural world here on Earth, there's always a story filled with adventure.